Praise for *Crash into Me*

"*Crash into Me* puts readers in the driver's seat with four
teens teetering on the edge of suicide. But will their cross-country
odyssey push them all the way over? Only the final page turn will
tell in Albert Borris's finely crafted tale of friendship forged from
a desperate need of connection. An exceptional first novel."
—**Ellen Hopkins**, bestselling author of *Crank*

"Take a bathroom break and be sure you have a few
free hours because from the moment you open this book you're
going to be on the ultimate heartbreaking, poignant road trip
to a place you never thought you'd go."
—**Todd Strasser**, bestselling author of *Give a Boy a Gun*

"Albert Borris is a powerful and insightful new voice
in young adult fiction."
—**Neal Shusterman**, author of *Unwind*

crash into me

Albert Borris

Simon Pulse

NEW YORK LONDON TORONTO SYDNEY

SIMON PULSE

An imprint of Simon & Schuster Children's Publishing Division

1230 Avenue of the Americas, New York, NY 10020

First Simon Pulse paperback edition July 2010

Copyright © 2009 by Albert Borris

All rights reserved, including the right of reproduction

in whole or in part in any form.

SIMON PULSE and colophon are registered trademarks of Simon & Schuster, Inc.

Also available in a Simon Pulse hardcover edition.

For information about special discounts for bulk purchases, please contact Simon & Schuster Special Sales at 1-866-506-1949 or business@simonandschuster.com.

The Simon & Schuster Speakers Bureau can bring authors to your live event. For more information or to book an event contact the Simon & Schuster Speakers Bureau at 1-866-248-3049 or visit our website at www.simonspeakers.com.

Designed by Mike Rosamilia

The text of this book was set in Adobe Garamond Pro.

Manufactured in the United States of America

10 9 8 7 6 5 4 3 2 1

The Library of Congress has cataloged the hardcover edition as follows:

Borris, Albert.

Crash into me / Albert Borris. — 1st Simon Pulse hardcover ed.

p. cm.

Summary: Four suicidal teenagers go on a "celebrity suicide road trip," visiting the graves of famous people who have killed themselves, with the intention of ending their lives in Death Valley, California.

ISBN 978-1-4169-7435-2 (hc)

[1. Emotional problems—Fiction. 2. Sex—Fiction. 3. Drug abuse—Fiction. 4. Self-esteem—Fiction. 5. Family problems—Fiction. 6. Seattle (Wash.)—Fiction.]

I. Title

PZ7.B6484956 Cr 2009

[Fic]—dc22

2008036225

ISBN 978-1-4169-9827-3 (pbk)

ISBN 978-1-4169-9579-1 (eBook)

To Cathy, my friend,
for whom I still write

Crash into Me

The third time I tried to kill myself

I used a rope. I picked the clothesline from the basement. I figured the cord didn't have to be real strong because I wasn't going to drop off a bridge or from a tree. I needed it just strong enough to kill me.

I've tried to kill myself six times; seven if you count walking down the median strip near the trucks and thinking of jumping in front of them. I suppose that doesn't really count. I didn't do anything that time except walk and practice falling off the curb into traffic. Everyone (mostly my mom, the psychiatrists, my two counselors) says that if I wanted to die, I would pick more lethal methods. Rope, I think, is pretty lethal.

The car slows. Frank turns off the expressway.

The third try was my angriest, my most dangerous. I put

that thin white cord around my neck and tied a slipknot. Then I pulled it so tight that I pinched the skin on my neck and made myself pass out—but not die. I did end up with a bruise from rope burn that I couldn't explain away. I was in the psych hospital for ten days that time.

The car turns again onto a smaller road.

"How long until we can stop for the bathroom?" Jin-Ae moans from the front seat. Her voice squeaks.

"One minute," replies Frank.

I don't speak. I'm thinking about the rope and my third try, because this time I think I may use a rope again.

We turn into the parking lot. I spot Audrey inside Dunkin' Donuts. She bolts up from the table. I wondered if we would know her right away since she never posted her picture, but her crew cut, the buzz, is unmistakable. She knows us. I watch her grab her pack from the floor and zoom past the counter. Audrey slams out the door toward us.

"Bathroom?" Jin-Ae asks.

Frank nods. He turns off the engine. Jin-Ae opens her door, starts to step out but stops to watch Audrey. I like being in the backseat where I can watch them both. Outside, Audrey heaves her cup at the trash can. It misses. She doesn't stop, just keeps bounding toward the car.

"She's in a rush," Frank comments.

"Nothing like a four-way suicide pact to get you going in

the morning," Jin-Ae says. She's always a bit loud, angry, abrasive, something.

Audrey is at Frank's window. "Let's go," she says.

"Down, girl," replies Jin-Ae, finally stepping outside the car. "Gotta pee."

"Can't we get going? I hate this town," Audrey whines. She leans in to look at me. "A pleasure to meet you, Your Highness. You all look different in person."

"She's in a hurry," Jin-Ae says to Frank, mocking Audrey.

"Come on," Audrey replies. "Mush, dogs."

Frank seems to smile at that comment. "Couple minutes. We need to stretch a little," he says to Audrey. "Been driving for hours already."

Jin-Ae points to the purple scar across Audrey's forehead. "So that's what a frying pan can do."

Audrey grunts but doesn't answer.

Frank gets out, takes Audrey's bag, and walks to the trunk. Audrey climbs into the backseat, near me, without saying another word.

I scramble out. We use the toilets, and then load up on doughnuts, and head north. None of us talk. We know where we're going, and what's in store.

MAYBE I SHOULDN'T HAVE COME ON THIS TRIP. I DON'T EVEN want to talk to them. It's so much easier to talk to people on the computer. You don't have to look at their faces. You can walk away. You can write whatever you want and then turn the computer off. I like it that way. Farther away from people.

"I'm officially a runaway now," Audrey says, once we're on the road again.

"What?" says Jin-Ae, turning from the front seat to look at her. "No wonder you're in such a hurry. Are we going to have the cops after us? Amber Alert and all that crap?"

"Just kidding." Audrey shakes her head. "I left a note."

"Suicide note?"

"No. I told my mom that I needed time to get my head together, and that I was staying at a friend's house for a while. She'll call my cell phone and yell, but she won't call the cops."

Frank turns the music up loud. "She better not," he yells.

"Won't matter in two weeks anyway," I mutter. No one hears me.

"Then how'd you get away from the folks, Frank?" Audrey hollers. "You tell 'em you're going on the celebrity suicide road trip?"

"No need to shout." He smirks, turning the music down. "And I don't know what you mean. I'm home. Like I told you, my parents are in Germany for a month. My brother is supposed to be watching me. Told him to cover for me or I'd narc him out for his weed."

"Really?" says Jin-Ae, excited. She grabs his arm. "Extortion?"

"Nice," says Audrey. She rearranges herself in the backseat, turning sideways with her feet resting against my legs, which makes me a little nervous. I'm not used to being touched. "All right you two, how about it?"

Jin-Ae says, "Hang on." She bends down, shuffling through her pocketbook.

Audrey, in the meantime, opens a small bag and pulls out a CD. She taps Frank on the shoulder with the case. "Nirvana."

He shakes his head. "Not yet. You have plenty of time."

"Two weeks," I say. Again, it doesn't seem like anyone hears me.

Audrey mumbles something I don't understand, and drops the disc onto the front seat between him and Jin-Ae. Frank turns right, following the turnpike signs.

"Here," Jin-Ae says, handing Audrey a piece of paper. "Our itinerary." She smirks. I spot our high school letterhead. I lean over, rereading with Audrey the list of fifteen colleges and universities that she and I are supposedly visiting.

"Nice fake. Federal offense, but nice forgery anyway."

"Works because we're from the same town," Jin-Ae explains. Audrey hands the paper to me, stares at me as if I should talk. Finally I do.

"Jin-Ae talked my mom into the phony college tour,"

I say. "My dad is in California, but they don't talk to each other, anyway."

"I even convinced them that there was a fee," Jin-Ae says, "so we both have some money."

I thought Audrey would be impressed by that comment, but she doesn't seem to care. "How long until Boston?" she asks. We're back on the highway now. Jin-Ae adjusts the mirror on her visor. For a second, I can see her face. Then nothing but dark hair. Audrey pulls out a pack of cigarettes.

"Five hours," says Frank. Audrey leans forward, offering Jin-Ae and Frank a cigarette. Frank shakes his head. "Don't smoke in the car, okay?" Audrey snaps the pack closed and sits back, hard.

According to MapQuest, Forest Hills Cemetery in Jamaica Plain, now part of Boston, Massachusetts, is 294 miles from the Cherry Hill Mall in New Jersey. Pictures on Google show a massive castlelike exterior and gate. If we're lucky, we'll arrive before rush hour and before the cemetery closes for the evening. I'd hate for our first stop to include jumping fences, especially in the dark.

Audrey keeps talking. "So, Jin-Ae, why do you get to pick first? You say 'head north' and we just have to follow?"

I find myself answering before Jin-Ae can speak. "Audrey, it's best to start on the East Coast. Everybody gets one suicide."

"Oh," says Audrey, "that's a cute pun there, Fact Boy. Nobody kills themselves more than once, right?"

"We share any extras," says Frank, taking her attention away from me. No one seems to see me shrink.

"I should have picked two," Audrey says, sitting back, folding her arms across her chest. "Three, even."

"E. E. Cummings and Eugene O'Neill are also buried there," Jin-Ae offers.

"Good research," Audrey says sarcastically. "Who were they?"

"Poet and playwright."

"Suicides?"

"No." Jin-Ae taps her nails on the window, obviously irritated.

"Then why are we going to see them?"

"We're not," Jin-Ae rebuffs. "First stop is Anne Sexton."

Audrey looks at me, ignoring Jin-Ae. "Bring any of their poetry?"

I shake my head, then look away.

"Hell, Audrey," says Jin-Ae. "None of us probably ever read anything by them. Anyone?" Jin-Ae's nail points to each of us. No answers. "See."

"They're famous," Frank states.

"They're dead," says Audrey.

"Amen," replies Jin-Ae.

Celebrity Suicide Road Trip
List and Schedule

1. Anne Sexton—Boston, Massachusetts (Jin-Ae)
2. Hunter S. Thompson—Woody Creek, Colorado (me)
3. Ernest Hemingway—Sun Valley, Idaho (Frank)
4. Kurt Cobain—Seattle, Washington (Audrey)
5. Death Valley, California (end of the road)

Options and Side Excursions: Anyone else interesting who we agree on on the way.

IN SPITE OF FRANK, AUDREY LIGHTS A CIGARETTE. THE OTHERS don't seem to notice. Audrey takes a big, long drag and then blows smoke right into the front seat.

Jin-Ae reacts first. "What the hell?"

I feel the car jolt. Frank jams on the brakes, slowing us to the speed limit. Ahead, a state trooper cruises in the right lane. Frank obviously doesn't want a ticket. How strange, even when you plan to die, instinct can take over. Or maybe he just doesn't want the trip interrupted. Even so, we gain steadily.

Audrey lays back, real far, head moving below the window. She holds the cigarette out in front of her face. "I was gonna make us T-shirts," she says. "I thought that might be fun."

"Isn't that a bit over the top?" Frank mumbles around the bite of doughnut in his mouth.

"Are you crazy?" Jin-Ae snaps. I think she's talking to Audrey. "Put that out."

"I think we're all crazy," Audrey says, still smoking

Then the smell hits me. That is not a normal cigarette.

I think Audrey is holding a joint. I haven't seen one in real life; only pictures, like in health class or on TV, but I can tell, especially because of the smell.

Audrey peeks out the window again, mouths something that I can't make out, something she doesn't want the others to hear.

I shrug.

Again she moves her lips without a sound. This time I get it: cops.

"Out!" Jin-Ae says louder.

"Okay."

Jin-Ae unrolls her window, and I smell something sweet, maybe vanilla, one of the girls' perfume mixing with the smoke. Out of view, Audrey holds the joint in her left hand, tapping the lit end so it will stop burning. She stays hunkered down out of sight of the police.

"Navigator?" says Frank. He seems oblivious to the smell and the joint. A few doughnut crumbs fall from his chin. "You still have the directions?"

"He can't be navigator from the backseat," Audrey says. Again, she mouths something to me, asking something. I don't know what she means.

"Yes, Frank. I do," I reply. I brought downloads of maps, encyclopedia entries, everything. And the computer in my lap has a satellite connection.

"Well?"

"Stay north onto the parkway, next exit, toward New York," I say to Frank. Audrey looks up, making eye contact.

"Is that weed?" Frank blurts out. "You got to be kidding. Aud—"

"Everybody hush," Jin-Ae interrupts.

The trunk of the police cruiser rides next to Jin-Ae's door. In a second we'll be right alongside the patrol car.

"I like the idea of T-shirts," chimes in Jin-Ae, hair blowing in all directions. "And be totally cool."

Audrey grimaces. She turns her head, peeking outside. Then she looks at me, opens her mouth. In goes the joint.

Outside, the police car pulls level with us. I turn and look at the trooper, who is wearing dark sunglasses. Below the window and out of view, Audrey chews and swallows. The officer gazes toward me. I smile weakly.

"Has anyone ever been to Boston before?" Audrey asks. She's quite the talker. I wonder if that's from the joint. I wonder if you can get high by eating marijuana. I think I'll look that up later.

"Don't do that again, Audrey," Frank snaps.

"Fine," she replies. "It was my only one anyway. So answer the question. Ever been to Boston?"

"Yes," says Frank. He's from Westchester, New York; lives closer to Boston than all of us from Jersey.

"I haven't really been anywhere," says Jin-Ae. "We vacation at the Jersey Shore. And I've been to Philly. But not once to New York. Pisses me off. My parents came all the way from Korea, and I haven't gone anywhere except Baltimore on an eighth-grade class trip."

"When?" Audrey asks Frank, not commenting on anything Jin-Ae said. I spot a sign for the Tappan Zee Bridge.

"Seventh grade. My dad took us to see Red Sox–Yankees at Fenway Park."

"I'm really pissed off that the Red Sox won the World Series," Jin-Ae says. "I liked that they were cursed, heartbroken. I mean, I'm not a baseball person, but I believe in suffering. Bad luck. Bad life."

"Interesting attitude," snips Audrey. Jin-Ae's nails tap something again, making that rat-a-tat sound. In less than two hours I can spot how they might fight over the next weeks.

"I don't like that happy, celebrate crap. Life sucks. Why pretend it doesn't because you hit a ball with a stick better than some others? You give people false hope. People still die."

"Yeah," Audrey says. "But just because your life sucks

doesn't mean other people can't be happy. If they like baseball, they could be happy in Boston."

"Yankees fans weren't happy then," Frank says. He grabs something from the seat and tosses it, without looking, toward Audrey. She ignores him.

"That's totally ridiculous," Jin-Ae replies to Audrey.

"No. It's people being different than you," Audrey counters. "They don't live your life." If she's high, shouldn't she be giggly or happy?

"Baseball is made-up stuff. It doesn't matter. It's a game."

"Not if it makes them happy."

I reach over and pick up the thing Frank threw. It's a Yankees cap.

"It's grown men with weird hats, running around with part of a tree, and gloves on," Jin-Ae persists.

Audrey grins. "I'll agree with that. But they could be happy."

"They're just kidding themselves."

"Hey, there's the bridge," Frank interrupts.

Audrey snatches the cap from my hand. "Mine," she blurts, like a two-year-old. She pulls it down on her head.

The road winds down, curving, then out across the river. The bridge looms, looking miles long, stretching out then up over the water. I find myself holding my breath. A very cool sight. I hadn't thought about what else we might see other than the graves.

"When we get to the middle of the bridge, look to the right. You can see down river about twenty miles to New York," says Frank.

Audrey leans forward, puts her mouth against his ear. "When we get to the middle, you could stop the car. We could just all jump now."

His lips purse tightly together. Then I see him shake his head. "No. The deal was at the end."

"Oh yeah." She giggles. "Loyalty to the pack."

"Pact," says Jin-Ae, stressing the *t* at the end of the word.

"Suicide Dogs." Franks smiles, saying our name out loud for the first time. I like the sound, the family heritage.

"Woof, woof," Audrey barks into Frank's ear. He jerks sideways, and the car jumps a little.

"What the—"

"Just trying to save us gas money." Audrey laughs.

The sun reflects brightly off the water, making me squint. Sure enough, the skyscrapers appear, far away and a bit foggy, but there they are.

"I wonder," says Jin-Ae, "if you could see the Twin Towers before they fell."

"Probably," replies Frank.

I keep my eyes on the skyline as we head down the bridge and the buildings fade from sight.

"Do you think those people who jumped from the Towers—

like off the roof because it was burning—I mean, that's suicide, but does that count as suicide?" asks Jin-Ae.

"Intentionally taking your own life? Suicide," I say.

"Agreed," says Frank.

"Not much of a choice." Audrey pulls out a piece of licorice, starts chewing. "Any other happy topics for us?"

"This *is* a suicide club," replies Jin-Ae, chomping a piece of gum. "And speaking of which"—she opens the glove box—"sign this."

"What?" asks Audrey.

"Our deal."

Frank shakes his head and looks like he wants to say something, but doesn't.

Jin-Ae, I think, is the weirdest. She hands a pen to Frank. He signs the paper, on the dashboard, as he drives.

"So what's it say?" Audrey asks.

"No killing ourselves until the end. Then we all do it. Honor the pact."

"Honor the pack," I whisper.

She hands me the pen and paper. I sign my name, then print "Owen" in capital letters next to my signature. Audrey snatches it, roughly. "Want me to sign in blood?" she asks Jin-Ae.

"If you want."

"You're cold."

Jin-Ae turns to face us from the front seat. Her eyes don't blink at all. "To quote, 'Beauty is at its most poignant when the cold hand of Death holds poised to wither it imminently.' Jacqueline Carey."

"So what?" Audrey counters. "Smart and cold. Hell, cold because you're smart."

Jin-Ae laughs. "Well-read."

"Whatever, just don't be all Shakespeare on us for the whole trip, okay?"

"Don't be illiterate, either."

Now that we're together, going somewhere in the car, it feels like a family. Maybe what a family should feel like, at least. Sharing. Talking. I don't really know, which is weird. I don't know what to say to them.

Audrey stares at Jin-Ae, holds the paper out in front of her, and then bites it. For a second she admires the teeth marks. She drops the contract on the front seat next to Jin-Ae. "Consider that my mark. Us modern illiterates prefer it to an X."

Maybe I should say how it all began.

Like this, in an instant message:

Jin-Ae: hey owen. that u?
Owen: yes
Jin-Ae: i told u i'd IM u when i got out

Owen: when was that?
Jin-Ae: 3 oclock today

School sent both of us to Hastings Hospital on the same day, back in February, for different things. She had her arms all cut up, sliced. They sent me because I wrote a poem about dying. When the intake counselor at Hastings asked about the last time I tried to kill myself, I told him about how I tried to smother myself with the plastic bag in my closet. They decided to admit me to the psych unit. I'd been to that fourth floor before. This time, when I got upstairs, Jin-Ae was there.

"You go to West, don't you?" she asked, walking right up to me before I'd even gotten to my room.

She's like that. In your face. Except with her family.

FRANK DRIVES FAST, AT LEAST FOR ME. I CAN SEE THE SPEED-ometer, and the needle is hovering around seventy-five. He drives faster than I'm used to, and that is a little scary, only I don't say anything. My mother drives slower, and we're hardly ever on the highway.

Even though we know one another online, it feels new getting to know them in person. I keep looking at Audrey's head and wondering what it would be like to be a girl with a buzz cut, especially with a big scar. Jin-Ae's hair is so straight, so black, like most Asians, only I hope I'm not stereotyping. Frank's different than I'd expected, lankier and more messy. I keep thinking someone should comb his hair.

WE MADE A LIST:

Top Ten Bizarre Ways to Kill Yourself

10. Walk in front of a subway car.

9. Put a plugged-in hairdryer in the bathtub with you.

8. Starve yourself to death in jail.

7. Cut yourself, then swim in the ocean with sharks.

6. Jump into a volcano.

5. Pay someone to beat you to death.

4. Lock yourself in a freezer.

3. Smash yourself in the head with a frying pan (like Audrey).

2. Stick yourself with a thumbtack ten thousand times.

1. Froot Loops and Drano.

AFTER FOUR HOURS EVERYONE GETS FUSSY. JIN-AE TAPS HER NAILS A lot, on the window or the door handle. Frank holds the wheel real loose, sometimes only with his fingers. Audrey wiggles her toes inside her pink socks (shoes off), and isn't afraid to move around. She puts her feet under her, on the seat, on the headrest, on the window. The girl has jitters.

We make it through Boston and to the cemetery quicker than MapQuest says. The gate looks like it's from medieval England. The graveyard is fancy, fancier than any I have ever seen.

"This is it," says Jin-Ae, stretching.

When we drive through the gate, the place seems to go on and on, so big and perfect. Not like the little cemeteries I went to before, in Cherry Hill. At home, graveyards don't look anything like this one. We see a sign with an arrow: OFFICE.

"They have an office?" Frank sounds surprised.

"Someone has to mow the grass and schedule the burials," Jin-Ae points out.

Off to the right, down past a row of headstones, is a small building, like a minihouse. Frank parks directly in front.

Audrey bolts out the door once Jin-Ae has climbed out; I'm stiffer and slower.

I can't imagine that the office gets many visitors like us. We're visiting our suicide family—our people. I imagine other people have real families here. I like the quiet. Gravestones are just that—stones. I like looking at them, rocks and grass, like they're part of nature. I take my time and am last going in the door.

Inside, Jin-Ae talks to the woman near a desk, whose soft voice fits the solemn job. "We have several maps."

"Do you have a lot of people come here then?" Jin-Ae asks.

"Sometimes," the woman replies. "It goes in spurts." I notice her glasses and old hair, and by that I mean the kind of hair that young people don't have—poofy, up, a weird color of white and brown. I wonder if she has dead relatives in here. And then I wonder if she thinks she'll die and be buried here.

"Bathroom?" Audrey interrupts.

The woman looks at her, pausing for a second, then points toward the back. "Coed, only one." Audrey nods and half-smiles.

"Could you tell us where to find her?" Jin-Ae continues.

A few minutes later, we're back in the car with directions to Anne Sexton's grave. Frank starts the car. As he backs up, I notice the decorations. Some of the graves are quite partylike. I've never seen anything like that before: wind chimes, a few birdhouses, Mardi Gras beads draped over the stones. Frank and the others don't seem to notice or care. One stone has a face engraved on the front. Maybe it's the dead person. Small picket fences surround two plots. The weirdest thing—a grave with forty little pinwheels sticking in the ground. They're all the same faded blue, not moving because there's no wind.

"Nice touch with the school-report thing," Audrey says, tapping Jin-Ae's shoulder.

"People like to help. No, actually, people need to help," says Jin-Ae. "Put yourself in a vulnerable position, and people jump right in to help. That's messed up. I mean, we could be going there to dig up Anne Sexton's bones, and that lady in the office would help us shovel."

As we turn toward the back part of the cemetery, I notice the big mausoleums—buildings of stone. A few with crosses on top. That makes me think of the three little pigs and the wolf trying to blow the houses down: straw, sticks, and these stone tombs.

Audrey nods. "I agree. People are easy to manipulate."

"I read about some famous guy's bones being stolen," says Frank.

"Who?" asks Audrey.

Frank shakes his head. "I forget. An old famous guy. From television."

I never find people easy to manipulate. Maybe that's a girl thing. I think it's very hard to get people to do what you want. I'm not very good at getting people to do what I want. I'm not very good at anything.

Anne H. Sexton, 1928–1974. Her grave marker is simple, set off from the road about fifty feet, in a line with all the others. She's buried with two other people, or at least their names are on her stone: George and Joan. We walk down a small path, over the grass, and stand looking at her grave site. I suppose I should write something about her later, but there's nothing I can think of that seems important. She's dead.

"Now what?" Frank asks, placing his hand on the tombstone.

"We're here," Jin-Ae starts, "because she was a famous poet."

"Dead poet," chimes in Audrey.

"She won the Pulitzer Prize for Poetry."

"Is there a Pulitzer for Suicide?" Audrey asks.

"We should do a little ceremony," says Jin-Ae, exhaling, obviously irritated with Audrey's interruptions. "Everybody sit down. I brought a poem."

"Serious?" Audrey whispers. Jin-Ae nods, and I spot the book in her right hand. We sit on the grass. Jin-Ae stays standing.

"Remember how I wanted to see Sylvia Plath's grave?" Jin-Ae begins. "Well, she's buried in England, but I found a poem by Anne Sexton called 'Sylvia's Death,' about Sylvia Plath's suicide, so I thought that would be good."

I'm surprised. First of all, that Jin-Ae has brought a book of poems and planned something here at the grave. I haven't done anything like that, although there is plenty of time before we get to my choice. Second, I don't like the poem. Kind of boring.

"I don't get it," Audrey says when Jin-Ae finishes.

"You don't always get poetry, Audrey. Not everyone understands what other people feel."

Audrey stands. I feel the grass under my palms and wonder

how badly Anne Sexton's corpse has deteriorated. "Well, I don't understand that poem too much at all," Audrey continues. "I guess I'm not very poetic. Not well-read."

As they are talking, I stand and walk over to a grave a few feet away. The headstone is reddish. On the top are a few small pebbles.

"I know why you picked her," Frank says, still sitting on the grass. "She's like you, sort of. A writer. Unhappy. Wishing she had someone who understood her. That's what killed her—being lonely."

"Poison or a rope is what killed her," Audrey comments.

"Carbon monoxide," I whisper. None of them seems to hear me.

I walk back over. "Jewish people put stones on graves when they come visit," I say. No one reacts. I kneel down. With my fingers I pull a clump of grass from the ground. Then start to dig. I find a tiny pebble about the size of my pinky's fingernail.

Frank leans back on the grass and keeps talking to Jin-Ae. "You know what I mean. Anne Sexton wrote all of her stuff down, in poems, like you write things down in your journal."

"Easy on the psychoanalysis, Frank," Jin-Ae replies.

I balance the stone on top of Anne Sexton's marker. Then I reach over for the book, which is titled *Live or Die*. So fitting.

"Look at that grave," says Audrey, pointing to an older

stone nearby. "Nineteen sixty-three. No stones, Owen." She must have heard me. "Think anyone comes to visit that person?"

"Probably not," says Frank.

"What's the point in having a gravestone then?" asks Audrey.

That's when I start to cry. I don't know why, but I do.

They want to talk to me, but I just walk back to the car. I don't say anything.

LATER, AS FRANK WINDS US OUT OF THE CEMETERY, AUDREY says, "I don't want to be buried. When it's all over, I want to be cremated. Thrown in the Wishkah River, like Kurt. Make sure you put that in there, Owen."

I hold the computer on my lap.

"You gonna write all the way to Seattle, Owen?" asks Jin-Ae.

Audrey leans forward, touches Jin-Ae's shoulder. "Cut him a break."

I still feel sad about the cemetery.

February 21

Jin-Ae: *u know any of the kids who killed themselves here in town?*

Owen: *no*

Jin-Ae: *i did. one. from East. we went to grade school*

together. i heard that he did bad on his SATs and that's
why he killed himself

Owen: pressure to succeed academically is a big suicide
factor but the main reason teens kill themselves is a
break-up

Jin-Ae: i coulda told u that without the textbook talk. how u
know that anyway?

Owen: study it

GOING TO VISIT SOMEONE'S GRAVE IS A WEIRD IDEA AND AN interesting experience. Before we started on this trip, back right around Memorial Day weekend, I went around town to a few cemeteries so that I could get the experience. Of course, I didn't take anyone with me, because that would have been really hard to explain. (I should have invited Jin-Ae, but I didn't think of it for some reason, probably because I never see her in school.) I think that was just before we made our pact.

The first cemetery I visited is the one I walk past every day on the way to school, the little one on the corner with no headstones, only tiny markers in the ground. That cemetery reeks of old. No new burials in more than one hundred years. That's more like a museum. I wonder if anyone would notice if they got rid of the place. I walked through the graveyard instead of past it on the sidewalk that day. I've never seen one person in there, not even to cut the grass. The letters in the stone are all fading and hard to read. The names are also different than ours, ancient names like Stanley, Agnes, Martha. I touched a lot of those stones and the faded letters. I wondered if any of the people killed themselves. Not like suicide would be carved on the stones, but I wondered. Or, I thought, did they have CSI technology to figure out why people died? Maybe a lot of suicides looked like accidents back then.

I think that was when I decided to kill myself by jumping in front of a truck. I could pretend to fall onto the highway and that way, as an accident, no one would feel really bad.

My two counselors always say things, like, "How do you think your brother James would feel if he found you dead?" Mr. Clark, the school counselor, always asks about my mom. "What about your mother?" I think she would feel bad and sad if I died, of course, but worse if she knew I killed myself. So I think that a fake accident would take away the guilt, maybe. My therapist, Sherri, she wants me to think about the other kids at school, because so many people in my town have committed suicide.

The trucks . . . That was the only time since we started the Suicide Dogs that I tried to kill myself. I walked out of the cemetery and didn't go to school. Instead I hiked through the woods and out onto Route 38. I walked along that grassy median strip in the middle between the two lanes of traffic all the way down to the mall, three or four miles. I kept thinking: All I have to do is fall off the curb. I practiced stumbling on the grass, falling down, forward, sprawling, flopping, and landing on the dirt and weeds as the cars drove past. I wanted a truck, a big tractor-trailer, speeding along faster than the speed limit, in the passing lane. That's all I wanted, a fast truck to fall in front of and be done.

But none came that morning.

About a half mile before the mall, I saw a pile of gray fur on the side of the road. I knew right away it was a dog. The thing looked like one of those little lap dogs, the kind old people keep, because they have nothing else in their lives. I sat down on the grass in the middle of the highway, and stared at that dog as the cars drove past. No one cared or noticed, not about that little dead thing, not about me. I wondered if the old lady missed her dog or if she knew what happened to it. Then I thought maybe the dog killed itself. Maybe not intentional suicide, but by accident, wandering around lost and without a purpose because the old person died.

Dogs are loyal like that; it's how they love. They can't help themselves.

When I finally got to the mall, I walked inside and bought a soda. Then, I wondered for a long time why no trucks drove in the fast lane that day.

February 22

Jin-Ae: how come i never see much of u in school?

Owen: im only in 10th grade. u r in 11th

Jin-Ae: did u know the kid who killed himself in 12th grade

Owen: no

Jin-Ae: me either. its weird to meet you in the hospital not the cafeteria

FRANK LETS AUDREY PUT IN HER NIRVANA CD AS WE LEAVE Boston.

"Couldn't you have brought an iPod?" asks Jin-Ae.

"Mine got stolen."

"Me too," says Frank.

Audrey turns up the music. That gets my thoughts rolling again, in spite of her singing along.

I think it must be quiet to be dead. It's calm in the cemetery, even if there are cars driving past. I wish I could have that kind of silence. Even though I don't always talk, there are a lot of voices in my head, or maybe it's my own voice that doesn't ever seem to stop. Even if the music is real loud.

IT's DUSK NOW. FRANK DOESN'T WANT TO STAY NEAR the cemetery, so he heads west across Massachusetts. The conversation turns to motels and stopping for the night.

"I have a credit card," Frank says. "My dad's." Again, I

notice the speedometer's needle near seventy-five. "I'll do gas, food, whatever."

"Maybe," Jin-Ae says, "we shouldn't start a paper trail yet since we've got a runaway."

"What if we go to a campground and park there?" says Audrey. "Cheap. Showers. One of us can pay cash."

"We don't have a tent, do we?" asks Jin-Ae.

Audrey shrugs. "Don't need one. Sleep in the car."

"Actually," says Frank. "I brought a tent. Says it sleeps three but really sleeps two. It's one of those pop-up kinds. All you do is pull the plug and it, like, pops up."

Jin-Ae bangs her head, purposefully, back into the head-rest. "You have got to be kidding."

"Nope," he replies. "Part of the adventure."

"Campground it is then!" Audrey leans back, feet on the seat again.

"Where do we find one?" asks Frank. "I'm beat. This has been a lot of driving."

"Maybe you should share that job." Jin-Ae grins.

Frank lets out a half-hearted laugh.

"I'll find one," I say. I feel really smart in the back with the laptop. "I downloaded all sorts of things about Massachusetts before we left. Plus, satellite Internet."

"Maybe Owen really can navigate from the backseat," says Jin-Ae.

I feel myself smiling, which is a funny sensation. "Give me a minute." I find a Web site, and then a campground. "Montague, Massachusetts. About forty-five minutes away. Twelve dollars for a weeknight tent site. With showers. Camp store."

"Go Owen," says Jin-Ae.

The smile feels deeper. I haven't felt important to anyone in a long time.

February 27

Jin-Ae: do u remember that kid robert from when we were at hastings? i think he got there when you were leaving the hospital

Owen: i'm not sure

Jin-Ae: he's from maple shade. really short. looks like he's about 10 yrs old

Owen: yes. y?

Jin-Ae: b/c he found both of his grandparents, dead

Owen: wow

Jin-Ae: he went over to their house and they were both in bed dead from sleeping pills. he called 911

Jin-Ae: cops came before the ambulance

Jin-Ae: he figured out that they killed themselves then he stole the police car. he's only 12

Owen: no

Jin-Ae: yes. he crashed into the pharmacy down at the end
*   of his street. on purpose*
Owen: i heard that story on the news not at hastings. that
*   was him?*
Jin-Ae: yes. he freaked out. said he wanted to die too. that's
*   y he went to hastings*
Owen: did he stay long?
Jin-Ae: longer than me
Jin-Ae: i bet that cop's in trouble for leaving the keys in the
*   car. i saw the drug store. big mess of bricks. he hit the*
*   wall. saw it when i got out*
Owen: he didn't look hurt when i saw him
Jin-Ae: air bags
Owen: suicides run in families you know
Jin-Ae: he was upset but he still has a chance b/c he's not
*   too old, like us*
Owen: u can be young and still want 2 die
Jin-Ae: i bet he didn't really want to die anyway. just get
*   over the pain.*

I'M VERY TIRED BY THE TIME WE PULL INTO THE CAMP. NONE of us wants to unpack the trunk and pull out the tent, especially since the sun has set. Instead, Frank simply parks the car in our spot, near the showers. They all climb out, but I close my eyes and lean over on the window. Later, I hear them come back and say something about food, but I'm too tired to reply. Even later, I hear the radio, a baseball game. The only time I stir is when Audrey's feet flop across my legs.

I DREAM OF MY FATHER. HE YELLS AT ME, ONLY I DON'T understand what he is saying. I am a little kid.

My father's mouth opens. Fangs sprout.

Suddenly I'm awake. Audrey's feet rest near my face. I feel cold, wishing I had a blanket. Something tastes sweet in my mouth. I realize, slowly, that I've bitten the inside of my cheek. Blood.

"Need some more room?" Audrey whispers, moving her feet.

I didn't realize she was awake. I mumble, pretending I am more asleep than I am. She doesn't say anything else.

"WHAT'S ONE THING YOU WOULD LIKE TO DO BEFORE YOU DIE?" Jin-Ae asks from the front seat. She bites into a doughnut.

"That's easy!" shouts Audrey. "Go to Seattle!"

We're back in New York now, done with Massachusetts and heading south toward Interstate 80, where we'll travel west for a week. The hills are winding, not like South Jersey.

"You're so predictable," says Frank. His hair sticks out sideways, messy from sleeping.

"She asked."

"True." He nods. "Is this like a last-chance question,

Jin-Ae? Like we should be stopping somewhere for your final burger?"

She ignores him. "You're a freak, Audrey. You know that, don't you?" Her tone is soft, friendly, muffled a bit by the doughnut in her mouth.

"Ain't we all?" Audrey sings a few lines of a Nirvana song. "'Load up on guns. Bring your friends.'"

Jin-Ae rolls her eyes.

I sip a diet soda; breakfast, sort of. The sun feels bright. I wish I had sunglasses.

"Seriously," Jin-Ae continues, "of all the things in the world, what would you do?"

"I am serious. Out of anything, I want to go to Seattle."

"I don't think there's much left there anymore," says Frank. "I mean, not the music. How long has Kurt Cobain been dead?" I feel myself staring. On the outside, he seems so normal. Like, why is he here with us? I guess that makes him the scariest.

"April 5, 1994," Audrey replies, shifting again, reaching for a doughnut from the front seat. "My birthday."

"Freak!" shouts Jin-Ae. "You know all this stuff, for real?"

"Yup. Besides, I'm no freakier than the quiet kid sitting next to me who knows every stupid fact on the planet about suicide." Audrey leans back, food in hand. "Wait." She lays her doughnut on the seat. She pulls off her sweatshirt. Underneath is a gray T-shirt with Kurt Cobain's face.

"See this?" she asks, exposing her left shoulder to me. She's so lean. "That"—she points to a small mark on her upper arm—"is where I burned myself on the anniversary of Kurt's death this year."

Frank turns and looks for a good second before turning back to the road. Jin-Ae barely glances at her. To me, the mark looks like a pimple scar or a birthmark, but I don't say anything.

Frank runs his fingers through his hair, not noticing the crumbs that stick to his scalp. "So what's your last wish, Owen?"

Traffic, I see, travels as fast as Frank, a regular seventy on the highway.

"I can't think of anything," I say.

"Quiet boy speaks," says Audrey.

Jin-Ae turns to look at me. "You mean that, Owen?"

I shrug.

"Nowhere to visit, go, something before the end?"

I shake my head. "Not really. I mean, this trip is pretty cool."

"Anything to get out of my town," Audrey mutters.

"I'd like to go to a football camp," Frank volunteers.

"I thought you didn't like football." Jin-Ae picks her fingernail into her doughnut, carving, like a knife. Her nails are all sharp points.

"No, I like it. A lot. I'm just not good. I'm not motivated. Or strong enough. I know a lot about football—statistics and plays and all—but I suck at it. I'm not coordinated enough."

"So you want to go to football camp and get better?"

"No!"

"You just said—"

"No." He turns around for a second, face flush. "I want to go to a pro-football camp. Check them out. The good players. See what that's like."

"Road, Frank." Audrey grimaces.

Frank turns back to the road, still talking. "Running drills. Most of the teams let fans watch. I'd like that."

"That's kind of a surprise," says Jin-Ae.

An idea crosses my mind, but I decide not to say anything. Lots of times I don't say anything. Frank nods his head and mumbles.

For a moment we're quiet, and I realize that the radio isn't on. We pass by a red tractor trailer. The kind of truck I wanted to hit me when I was practicing killing myself by falling off of the curb. The thought passes through my head that Frank could kill us all by driving into or under that truck. A very short trip.

"What about you?" Frank asks Jin-Ae.

Jin-Ae turns to look out the window at the truck. "I'd like to get laid," she says.

Audrey laughs out loud. "Hello!"

I'm speechless.

"I'd like to know what it's like."

"Thought you were a lesbian," says Audrey.

"I am. But I've never done it."

"Me either," Frank comments softly.

"Good lord. I'm the experienced one here?" Audrey says, voice rising. "I thought I was supposed to be the young one."

After another quiet minute, Audrey says, "Owen?"

I don't answer. I feel heat in my neck and my ears. I don't want to tell her that I've never had a girlfriend, never kissed anyone, not once, not even at a party in seventh grade or on a dare. I'm embarrassed of being a prude.

"Damn," Audrey says, when none of us talk again. "Then I'm the ho of this group. I've been with more than one person, and, let's just say, people said I was cheap."

"We don't care about that," I say.

She turns to look at me, brown eyes wide. "That's sweet, lover boy, and I don't care. Jin-Ae, maybe one of these guys can help you out sometime before the big event."

I don't know how serious Audrey is about the sex stuff. I don't really know how to tell about other people. I'm also embarrassed. Between the front seat and the door, I spot Jin-Ae's hand on the door armrest. She's digging her fingernails into her other hand now, on the outside, like she's trying to carve something into her hand and not the doughnut. I can tell she's upset. Mad or sad or embarrassed. I want to say something, but don't know what, so I don't say anything. What else is new?

No one speaks for a long time. Audrey nags Frank about playing more Nirvana.

"Please," she whines.

"It's so old." He groans.

I don't care; it's new to me. Franks nods his permission, and Audrey hands Jin-Ae another CD. We pass through the tolls for the Tappan Zee Bridge again. New England is behind us for good, forever, till death do us part.

"Didn't they send you to Hastings because you were going to jump off a bridge, Owen?" asks Jin-Ae. Traffic slows Frank's driving to fifty as we head up onto the Tappan Zee.

I squirm a little. "No. I *wrote* about jumping off the Ben Franklin Bridge. But they put me in Hastings because I tried to suffocate myself with a bag."

"Plastic?"

"Dry-cleaning."

"You know what?" says Jin-Ae, looking out the window. "I'd like to go to New York City before I die."

I follow her gaze south, down the Hudson River, and see the city skyline.

"How about it, Frank?" asks Audrey.

He grins. "Sure, get me directions."

I do more than that.

February 28

Owen: research says boys use immediate and angry techniques
   like guns or car crashes—things where you can't be saved
Jin-Ae: u really do know all this, don't u
Owen: girls pick slower ways, like pills—with time for them
   to be rescued
Jin-Ae: u r smart enough. u should be sharing this with
   other people
Owen: ?
Jin-Ae: i know a few suiciders on line. join a chat?
Owen: no thanks

"WE CAN STOP," I SAY, "TO SEE JUDY GARLAND. TWO EXITS UP. Only about fifteen minutes."

"Suicide?" Jin-Ae pulls a brush from somewhere, and starts working on her hair, with long, regular strokes.

I nod my head. "Her official cause of death is accidental overdose. But they were just being polite."

Frank looks at me in the rearview mirror. "Dorothy, right?"

"*The Wizard of Oz*," answers Jin-Ae, brush still moving through her hair. "Mother of Liza Minnelli."

"All those in favor?" asks Audrey. She raises her hand. Frank puts his hand up. Jin-Ae starts to move her brush toward the car roof, but then reaches back and rubs Audrey's head real hard.

"Ahhh." Audrey grunts.

"Been wanting to do that."

"Say please, next time."

I raise my hand, making it unanimous, and Frank asks for directions.

THE ROAD TO FERNCLIFF CEMETERY IS QUIET AND EMPTY. I'M surprised how deserted the area seems this close to the city. All the information to find Judy Garland's grave is right online. Exact plot, everything. With most people, that's not the case. It takes more work and research.

Her final resting place is in a mausoleum called the "Cathedral of Memories." The door is gold, and inside the mausoleum is cooler than I expect.

"Awesome," Audrey says as we enter. Her voice echoes against the rows of plaques.

I'm surprised that the place is well lit, bright. I thought crypts were dark. I'm amazed to see windows, burning candles, a few electric lights.

Frank goes straight over to Judy Garland's crypt, number thirty-one. Audrey wanders around, touring, touching the different plaques with her hand. Jin-Ae stays near me.

"How'd she do it, Owen?" Even in a whisper, Jin-Ae's voice sounds loud.

"Overdose. Went to sleep."

Jin-Ae stares past me, listening but watching Frank at the same time. "Maybe we should all take pills at the end. Sleep in the desert. We never agreed on a final plan."

I shrug. Our feet sound loudly against the tiles. Jin-Ae raises her voice. "Hey, Frank. Did you put all your affairs in order before you left? You know, prepare?" I've heard that phrase before. "Affairs in order."

He rubs his fingers on the G in "Garland." "Cleaned my room, that's enough."

"You, Owen?" I look down. Doesn't seem like there is anything to put in order.

"I wrote a will," Jin-Ae says, answering her own question. "Left my books to the library, and my body to science."

"You're a strange one," Franks says.

Audrey steps near us now. "I wrote a will too!"

Jin-Ae looks at her.

"'Will you miss me?' In red lipstick on the bathroom mirror."

"For real?"

Audrey rolls her eyes. "'Course not." She breaks out singing. "'Somewhere'"—the sound ricochets off the stone, reverberating like a chorus—"'over the rainbow.'"

Jin-Ae turns to Frank. "Should we . . . ?"

He shakes his head. "At least it's not Nirvana."

One by one, Frank and Jin-Ae and me take seats on the

floor, backs against the stones. Audrey continues with her song, touching plaques and almost dancing. For the most part, she's tolerable, even though the high notes aren't easy for anyone. I guess I never really thought about that song and how sad it is, how lonely that girl is there on that farm in Kansas, so upset that her family doesn't understand her that she tries to run away. Audrey's voice, or maybe it's the crypt, makes the song depressing.

Jin-Ae talks quietly, for once, but not so softly that the singing drowns her out. "What do you think happened to Toto?"

"You mean the dog?" asks Frank.

"Yes."

"From the movie?"

"Yes. I mean, do you think it's in the crypt with her? Think Judy Garland killed it with herself? You know, put pills in the dog food?"

"Probably just a dog from the movie," he replies. "Probably not even hers to keep."

Audrey launches into the final lines of her song, louder and livelier. "'Why, oh why—'"

Her voice cracks. Jin-Ae winces. "She'll wake the dead."

"Funny," says Frank.

"'Can't I?'"

That's it.

Frank and Jin-Ae stand up. Audrey heads toward the door. No major revelation. Nothing magical to learn. Just an empty crypt with four kids inside. I wish I had an answer. I wish I even had a good question, something I could pretend Judy Garland might be able to answer. But, all I've got is "What happened to Toto? What happened to the dog?"

March 1

Jin-Ae: u wont believe wat hppned to the girl

Owen: ?

Jin-Ae: from my chat

Owen: what?

Jin-Ae: no way. join the chat & u can ask

NEW YORK CITY OFFERS A FAMOUS MURDER/SUICIDE STORY, OF Sid Vicious and Nancy Spungen. He stabbed her to death. I wonder, Does that count for our club? Sid was in a punk band called the Sex Pistols, and she was his groupie-turned-manager. Four months after she died, he overdosed on heroin, thirty times too much—an intentionally lethal dose. Sid's mother tried to bury him next to Nancy's grave in Pennsylvania. Nancy's mom said no. I can't tell if this is true or not, but one Web site says that Sid's mother went to Pennsylvania and threw his ashes on Nancy's grave. There's another rumor saying that Sid's mother dropped his ashes, accidentally, in Heathrow Airport, and now his ghost flies around the tourists.

I want us to visit them at the place where she died.

Room 100, Hotel Chelsea, New York City. I know lots about suicide, lots of places to go, people to see, ways to die. I brought so much with me on the computer. I feel like a spaceship navigator, on the *Enterprise* maybe, steering us around suicide galaxy.

"Would anyone want to visit more suicide places in the city?" I ask.

"That's why we're here, Professor," says Audrey, playfully sticking her feet toward my face.

"Whatever you want, Your Smartness." For a lesbian, Jin-Ae is cute. I mean, I think she is attractive. Of course, lesbians can be pretty. New York is her death wish, and I want to be nice to her, so I start looking through the tourist stuff that I've downloaded. I don't look up from the keyboard for twenty minutes, until we're on the George Washington Bridge. By then I have plans for our whole day.

March 1

Jin-Ae: pleeease owen. just join the chat.

Owen: idk

Jin-Ae: seriously, they r cool. i found franks myspace
    in december

Owen: but i don't know them

Jin-Ae: u don't have to say anything

Jin-Ae: owen, please

Owen: maybe

I THINK WE'RE ON THE PALISADES INTERSTATE OR THE EAST Side Highway. I don't know for sure. Maybe a GPS would have been a good idea.

"We could go to the Dakota, where John Lennon was shot," Frank says.

"No suicide involved." Audrey dismisses it quickly, before any of us can speak. "So we're not going." Her words sound like a command.

"Heath Ledger?" asks Jin-Ae.

Again, Audrey answers quickly. "Speculation. Accidental. Doesn't count."

"Elvis?"

"Also, accidental overdose."

"James Dean?"

"Car crash."

"Tupac?"

"Drive-by."

"Joan of Arc?"

"Oh, come on, Jin-Ae."

"Joan of Arc?" she repeats.

"Burned at the stake."

"Ah," says Jin-Ae, "but she could have lived if she confessed. Thus methinks this counts as suicide."

"Not in New York," counters Audrey. She turns to look out the window, ending the banter. Frank doesn't speak. He's concentrating, driving slower in all the traffic. The speedometer doesn't go above fifty. Jin-Ae looks like a tourist, staring out the window. Her fingernails aren't digging into flesh anymore, at least not that I can see.

New York is so different from Philadelphia, the city that I know best, even though I haven't been there in a long time. My mom took me to the Philadelphia Zoo and the baseball stadium with James, a few years ago. But only part of Philadelphia is big like New York, which is all giant buildings.

"I know my way around from Lincoln Center," Franks says. "We can park there. It's about Fifty-first street, Owen. Look up directions, okay?"

We must drive about a hundred blocks before we find Lincoln Center, which is in the middle of Manhattan. From there, Frank knows how to get us on the subway.

Frank, we came on this road trip because you wanted to visit Hemingway's grave in Idaho. Maybe that will help you feel better about life. If not, then maybe you can find a way to finally finish it off with Hemingway's help.

March 4
Jin-Ae: everybody describe yourself in 2 words
Audrey: y?
Jin-Ae: owen doesn't know u yet

Audrey: EZ. Nirvana freak

Frank: let me think for a minute

Audrey: Jin-Ae?

Jin-Ae: he knows ME!

Audrey: do it anyway

Jin-Ae: ok—smart. lesbian

Audrey: figures

Jin-Ae: no. intense. lesbian

Frank: athletic underachiever, i suppose

Frank: UNathletic

Owen: i can only think of one word

Jin-Ae: well?

Owen: lonely

JIN-AE STANDS AT THE RAILING, LOOKING TOWARD THE STATUE of Liberty. She's the only one of us who has never been to New York City.

I ask, "Do you know that Spalding Gray jumped off this ferry?"

We're gathered at the back of the ferry, heading for Staten Island, just to go there, then straight back to Manhattan. A kind of suicide ship ride.

"Never heard of him," says Frank.

"Me neither," I reply. "Just from the Web. He was an actor."

The skyline, all the silver and mirrors and the way the sun shines off of everything, looks great. I can't see Audrey's eyes because of her sunglasses, but I know she's disappointed about not being able to get into the room where Sid killed Nancy. That's the reason I've brought the watermelon.

I stand with it under my sneaker. The ashes of Audrey's cigarette fall, caught by the wind, and disappear. That makes me think of people who have jumped off bridges into this river, but who never get found. Vanished, like fish food. Like a celebrity nobody has ever heard of before.

None of them say anything about Spalding Gray. So I keep going. "He jumped off, maybe right here, and they didn't find him for two months."

"It's pretty cool out here," says Frank, although I don't know what he means by that. A good place to jump?

"Like this!" I shout really loud. The three of them turn to look at me.

I bend and pick up the watermelon. Then I heave it straight over Jin-Ae's head, out into the water. She ducks.

Whoom. The watermelon makes a huge splat.

"Whoa!" yells Frank.

I figured it would sink, but that watermelon bobs right back up to the top.

"Owen," Audrey says. "I wanted some of—"

"You can't do that!" A voice yells.

We all turn. Behind us, a woman in uniform stands, hands on hips.

Audrey gets cocky right away. I like that about her. "It's biodegradable," she says.

"It's litter," the uniform replies.

"That"—Audrey grins, pointing over the edge—"is a watermelon. Not litter."

"I don't care if it's nothing, that's bull," says the uniform.

"Well," Audrey counters, "he was going to jump, and I talked him into the fruit sacrifice."

Jin-Ae chuckles. I stare at her.

The uniform clenches her teeth. "Don't do it again."

Surprisingly Audrey holds her tongue. The lady leaves.

"I wasn't going to jump over."

"I know." Audrey smiles. She touches my arm, and I feel something burn.

The watermelon drifts away from us, behind the ship. I see it moving a little, reflecting the sun. I wonder if it's symbolic that it didn't sink. That's like me when I tried to drown myself in a way. Like maybe this isn't its time to die. Maybe things want to live.

It's so confusing. I keep thinking about how five kids in my town have killed themselves in three years. Five kids. And two adults. That's a lot. I'm sure it would be more if people didn't stop others. Like Jin-Ae and me. If things want to live, then why did those kids die? Why did Frank's uncle kill himself? Something about living and dying just doesn't make sense.

No answer from Spalding Gray. No answer from the watermelon. The Statue of Liberty just stands there, mute.

Top Ten Things to Remember about NYC

10. The subway, the A, the number 1. Dirt. Urine smell. Loud and noisy. Guy with no legs playing saxophone.

9. Sid Vicious. At Hotel Chelsea, we can't get in.

8. Ground Zero. Big death thing. Kind of strange.

7. Chinatown. All different foods. Audrey thinks bird's nest is a real bird's nest. Frank eats like a mess, sloppy.

6. The Naked Cowboy. A guy in his underwear playing guitar. Jin-Ae takes his picture with her phone.

5. Statue of Liberty. Cool.

4. 511 Yankees caps counted by Audrey.

3. Gay Bingo. Everyone in drag. The whole crowd shouted out, "O-Sixty-nine!" A sex joke. Other kids there, too. One asked if I was gay. Audrey said no for me.

2. Fifty-dollar bill that Frank grabbed, swirling in the wind, right out of midair.

1. Pigeon poop. One crapped right on Audrey's soda can as we were walking. Nobody could stop laughing.

WE'RE GOING TO NEW JERSEY FOR THE NIGHT. I FOUND US A campground in Long Branch, about an hour away. Frank's not tired, so he doesn't mind the drive. Audrey falls asleep first, in back with me. She has on pink socks again. I sleep with my sneakers on my feet.

THAT MORNING I'M THE LAST TO WAKE UP, STILL IN THE backseat. None of the others is anywhere to be seen. I'm hungry.

That's one thing we still haven't figured out yet, eating. We've stopped to buy junk food, but I think we should have some real food in the car to keep us going. Now that we're camping, maybe we could make breakfast together. I spot red licorice in the front seat and eat a piece.

I find Frank in the bathroom, buttoning his Yankees jersey after showering. I can't help but notice the acne on his neck and shoulders.

"We don't have any towels," he says. "None of us, even to share."

"We don't have any food, either," I reply.

"There's a little store here. We'll get something." He picks up his shoes and walks toward the door, remaining barefoot. "I think we all packed pretty lousy."

"Maybe we could buy stuff for the next couple days," I say, "so we don't have to worry about it as much."

"Okay."

As he leaves I decide to shower. I'll use my T-shirt to dry off. When I'm done, I head back to our campsite and find Audrey passing out orange juice and blueberry Pop-Tarts.

"Breakfast of champions, Owen." She smiles, offering me one of the Pop-Tarts. "Sleep well?"

I shrug and join them at the picnic table.

"You were a good pillow," she says. "These guys slept together in the tent. I mean, not slept together, but you know what I mean."

Frank looks cleaner and better than yesterday. Jin-Ae seems a bit sleepy still, dull. "I'm not sleeping in the tent again," she says. "Bugs. Noises. Rocks in my butt. I am not sleeping in there, I swear, never again. I hardly slept."

"Anyone want some Prozac?" Audrey says, opening a pill bottle and pouring something into her hand.

"Oh girl, I wouldn't take those. I hate the whole counselor take-this-pill-you'll-feel-better crap," says Jin-Ae.

"Whatever. They're my mom's prescription, anyway. I just stole 'em." She motions with her hand. Frank shakes his head no; Jin-Ae doesn't respond. I don't know if Audrey's serious. I wonder if they are really her mother's pills. I wave my hand, meaning none.

"I hope you're keeping a good list of all the dead people and suicide stuff we're seeing, Owen," Audrey continues, swallowing a pill or more. "We've got a pretty good start already. Sexton. Dorothy. That actor guy, and I think you should mark down Ground Zero."

"I'll make a list," I tell her.

Frank grabs another Pop-Tart from the box on the table. "Audrey thought we could go find Nancy Spungen's grave in Pennsylvania. It's west, at least."

"I couldn't find anything online about where it is, though," I say. "But I had another idea." Audrey is still wearing her pink socks. Maybe she only brought a few pairs. "I found something else online."

"What?" Audrey asks.

Jin-Ae picks up something and puts it in the trash. She's like that, tidy.

"The Eagles are holding minicamp at Lehigh University. Next three days. Maybe we could go that way."

"Football Eagles?" asks Audrey. She runs her hand over her buzz cut, then traces the scar on her head with her pinky. I watch Frank open his mouth a little.

"Yup. Football Eagles."

"And where exactly is Lehigh University?" she asks.

"Sort of on the way. Not exactly, but it's west and that's where we're going."

Frank hasn't said anything, but I can see his face, his eyes open a little bit more. I know he's excited.

"Training camp is August," he finally says, his voice braced for disappointment.

"Nope," I answer. "Says it right here. End of June. Voluntary precamp. Rookies."

"That's settled then," Audrey says before Frank can comment. "Football Eagles, here we come. Can't deny a dying man's last wish."

"I hate football." Jin-Ae tosses the crust of her Pop-Tart in the trash.

"This ain't about you," Audrey says. "We went to New York because of you."

"I didn't say we shouldn't go. I just said I don't like football."

"Suck it up, girlfriend."

I'm waiting for Frank to say something, then the girls realize that he isn't talking, either. We all turn to him. In that minute I know what he means when he says he isn't good enough. He's got this big mouthful of food, chewing real fast, with crumbs on his chin and his shirt. Even with showering just a few minutes ago, he's got dirt on his hands, or maybe it's charcoal from the fire pit. His legs are stretched out in front of him, and he looks like his body is too small for his limbs. I feel sorry for him.

"Frank?" Audrey prompts.

He grins and more crumbs fall out, but he's smiling and nodding happily. "Let's go."

We pack up.

When she's not looking, I grab Audrey's pills. Advil, not Prozac. I fold a Pop-Tarts wrapper around the bottle, then throw it in the trash.

March 6

Owen: *when did u all meet*

Audrey: *we havent in person. just on line. franks journal*

Owen: *oh*

Jin-Ae: *i keyworded suicide. myspace friends*

Frank: *that suicide thing was from 7th grade. almost 4 yrs ago*

Owen: *did u try to kill yourself*

Frank: *yes*

Owen: *how?*

Frank: *pills. i had to eat charcoal at the hospital*

Owen: *i took pills once too. didnt work*

ACCORDING TO MAPQUEST, CHERRY HILL TO BOSTON TO Woody Creek, Colorado, is 2,458 miles, thirty-eight hours and twenty minutes of driving. A long way. From there we go 698 miles to Sun Valley, Idaho, in just over twelve hours, then 656 miles to Seattle, about eleven hours. Then Death Valley, another 1,117 miles and nineteen hours. Then nothing. No more miles.

I have to recalculate the new mileage adding our New York City detour and the campground in Long Branch to Lehigh University in Pennsylvania. After that we'll go back to the regular itinerary. We should still make it to Frank's choice, Hemingway's grave, by July 2, the day he died.

We pull into a Wal-Mart in North Brunswick, New Jersey. After about two days of traveling, more than five hundred miles of driving, and we're still in New Jersey. Frank and Audrey go for food. Jin-Ae and I wander around looking for other things. "A towel or two," I say.

"We can share," she replies. "We need blankets or sleeping bags. Frank is the only one who brought anything. I've been using my clothes like pillows and blankets."

"What else do we need?"

We end up with aspirin, two big towels, and two cheap comforters (on special). We meet Audrey and Frank up front. They have more groceries than I imagined they might: pretzels, Pop-Tarts, bread, tuna fish, mayo, peanut butter, crackers, a hunk of cheese, a few cans of stew, chips, and two gallons of water.

"I'm going to charge it all," says Frank. "I don't care what my father says."

"It's not like you're going to be around when they get the bill," says Audrey.

That depends upon whether or not we actually all go through with the plan, our pact. Or whether we, or he, chickens out. Frank gets what she means. He hunches over, seems suddenly darker. He mumbles something.

Audrey stares at him. "What?"

"I'm not backing out," he repeats.

"Isn't this," Jin-Ae starts, "about finally—"

"Finally, what?" Audrey snaps, interrupting her.

Jin-Ae doesn't answer.

"Finally getting away from my mother, is what. At least for me," Audrey says, picking up the chunk of cheese, then dropping it back into the cart. "You all are so serious—seriously serious."

"A deal," I say, low enough so that I hope no one hears, "is a deal."

"Get whatever we need," Frank mumbles. "I don't care."

"For real?" says Audrey, mood different in a second.

Jin-Ae changes the subject. "What's with the hat?" Audrey is wearing Frank's Yankees cap pulled way down low, hiding her eyes.

She ignores Jin-Ae again.

Jin-Ae sighs loudly, disapproving, frustrated. Something.

We leave the two carts, split up, and go searching again. I want a pillow for the backseat, and a pair of sunglasses. I'm back first. Audrey returns with cheese that sprays out of a can, a box of maxi pads, and four packages of red licorice. In a few minutes Frank and Jin-Ae come back. She holds two pints of ice cream, paper plates, napkins, and plastic forks, kitchen stuff. Frank grips five permanent markers and a football.

"Are we going to picnic for every meal?" Audrey asks. Jin-Ae shrugs.

"Camping stuff," Frank says. "Anybody have any?"

Once more we head off into the store, this time staying together, gathering up a few candles, matches, flashlights, bug spray, two cheap sleeping bags, and a lantern.

Frank puts it all on his father's credit card. We pile back into the car, trunk brimming and backseat full, and head to Lehigh. We share the ice cream as it starts to melt. Frank and Jin-Ae pass one pint between them in the front. Audrey and I knock plastic spoons in the container in the back. I'm not really used to sharing anything.

March 8

Audrey: i need to share something with u all

Jin-Ae: wat?

Audrey: im not really 19

Jin-Ae: how old r u

Audrey: freshman—high school

Frank: 14 or 15?

Jin-Ae: sure ur not an old guy pedophile stalking us?

Audrey: 15 in April. u have to lie in order to get a myspace

WE CROSS THE DELAWARE RIVER ON INTERSTATE 80, A PRETTY place that doesn't look like New Jersey—big cliffs, woods, and the river.

"Bye, Jersey," Audrey says, tossing a piece of licorice out the window into the river.

It strikes me that we'll never be here again. Ever. I wonder if the others think the same thing. I don't say anything, but neither does anyone else.

Two hours later we stop at a market, and Frank buys beer with a fake ID. Jin-Ae wants vodka or whiskey, but we can only get liquor at the state store. (Pennsylvania is strange in that way.) Frank doesn't want to make an extra trip. He buys two six-packs of beer and four bottles of hard lemonade. We buy sandwiches and lunch stuff.

I haven't ever been on a college campus before, not with a big field and stadium. Because of the beer, we don't sit in the stands. Instead we sit on a hill and watch from the grass. The players are at lunch. Frank walks over to a group of guys near the concession stand.

"Perfect day for poetry," Jin-Ae says, sprawling on the lawn. She takes a bottle of hard lemonade and opens a book. I notice Audrey in long sleeves again, which would be too hot for me. Jin-Ae opens a bag of chips.

"Only quarterbacks and receivers," Frank says when he returns. "No pads."

He hands me a lemonade. I take a sip and find out why it's called hard—because of the liquor in it, whiskey. It tastes like crap, so I don't drink it. I spit it out. Jin-Ae laughs at me, but I don't care.

"Hard-core alcoholic," she mumbles. I pass my bottle to Audrey and take a few chips. Frank opens a beer, drinks the whole thing in one long sip.

"Andre Waters," Franks says, spitting the last few drops of beer.

"Huh?"

"Killed himself. Played for the Eagles a long time ago. But he was kind of a legend."

Audrey turns to me. "How'd you miss that one, Mr. President of the United Suicides of America?"

"Didn't," I reply.

She squints her eyes, not believing me.

I say, "He didn't die here or get buried here."

"No?"

"Florida."

"Nothing else to add?"

The question feels like a challenge. I tell her what I know. "The closest celebrity suicide is probably Abbie Hoffman."

"Oh yeah?"

"He killed himself in a turkey coop near New Hope. He was a hippie, who—"

"I know who he is!" Audrey snaps. We sit for a few moments

with nothing to do except watch Jin-Ae read her book.

The players come out by one o'clock. I thought the Eagles all wore green, but they wear different colors, like white and red. Frank explains that the quarterbacks wear red, so no one will hurt them.

"Do you want to walk up closer?" I ask him.

"No," he says, and sits back on the grass drinking beer after beer, really fast. I wonder if he will vomit.

Eventually he starts to yell things to the players. "Nice catch," he says. "Nice pass." Once he yells out, "Nice ass." Then he starts laughing really hard. I'm sure he meant "nice pass." We all laugh.

Eventually Frank falls asleep and so does Audrey. I watch the players run and catch, and Jin-Ae walks over to the shade to read. Normally I wouldn't do something like this but maybe the sip of lemonade has made me a little drunk. I take Frank's football and one of the markers, and I walk over to where the players leave the field. A few of the popular players have big crowds around them, fans wearing green jerseys. I don't go all the way near them. Instead I walk over to the fence at the edge, near midfield. I stand by myself. A handful of players, probably the second string, keep running plays. I wave to one when he comes sort of close. Amazingly he comes over and signs the football. I don't know who he is because the shirts don't have names on the back. I don't recognize him, and he doesn't say who he is, either. I can't read his handwriting. Maybe Frank won't care about his name, anyway.

March 10

Audrey: we need to have a name

Jin-Ae: ?

Frank: like suicide anonymous?

Audrey: too emo

Frank: y do we need a name?

Audrey: b/c i think it'd be cool and i want one

Frank: u don't like suicide anonymous?

Audrey: no. too much like AA. my dad tried that. and if he
    tried it i don't want to do it. what about suicide club?
    like the movie, Fight Club

Jin-Ae: great flick

Audrey: u guys?

Frank: fine by me

Audrey: we keep it secret, right? nobody talks about
    fight club

Owen: k

Frank: i'm in

Jin-Ae: i dunno about the name tho. suicide club sounds
    kinda 4th grade.

Audrey: come up with something better then.

By four o'clock the practice field is empty. I wake Audrey with a shake. She touches her face, which is bright red, and moans. "Ouch!" she cries. "You shouldn't have let me burn."

Her voice wakes Frank. He is plastered. "Play ball!" he shouts. That is just the start.

We carry and walk him back across the field and then the parking lot to the car. He's an awkward, big, stupid drunk. He can't walk. He keeps falling over onto one of us. Audrey is the smallest, so we give her stuff to carry while we try to help Frank. In the middle of it Jin-Ae's phone starts to ring. She yells out, "Oh hell."

Of course she doesn't answer the phone.

Frank mumbles "My father is an alcoholic" out of nowhere.

"Welcome to that club," Audrey says.

Then Frank starts crying as we're walking. "I don't want to turn out like him."

Audrey, walking behind us, starts talking real loud to Frank, which is bad. He keeps turning his head around to try and talk back to her. That makes it harder to keep him moving to the car.

"No one wants to turn out like their parents," Audrey says.

"No, I mean it." He moans, fighting against my hand on his arm.

"We heard you. You don't have to, Frank."

"Yes, I do," he cries, tears on his cheeks now. "I'm cursed. There's, like, no way out of my family."

"Just live your own life," Audrey suggests.

"I can't!" he shouts.

That's when he turns around, real quick, and slaps me in the face with his hand, maybe his elbow. I don't think he knows that he did it; an accident.

My nose stings. I let go of Frank. My hands go to my face. Frank flops, twisting, and falls onto the ground, feet pointing one way, face looking back at Audrey.

Drunks don't always make sense, I guess. I haven't been around many of them. They change subjects and say stupid things. They fall down.

"You have a great ass, Jin-Ae," Frank mumbles.

I don't think she hears him. Frank reaches toward her butt, but misses. "Hey, if I think a lesbian is cute," he shouts, "does that make me gay?" Audrey laughs.

"What a mess," Jin-Ae says. "Let's get him up. Owen!" I'm surprised by her tone. "Owen!" she yells again.

"What?"

"You have a bloody nose!"

She's right. My shirt is red and I can feel the wet on my lips and chin now.

"We better get to the car," Audrey advises. "I have a feeling this is going to keep getting better and better. I'm still buzzed a little."

"I'm sorry, Owen," says Frank, still on the ground.

I pull up my shirt and grab my nose to stop the bleeding. We wander toward the car. Jin-Ae helps Frank, with Audrey on the other side carrying him and one of our blankets and the football. I'm holding the other blanket, along with my nose. At least till we get to the parking lot, when the bleeding finally stops.

Jin-Ae says, "I'll drive."

Frank doesn't say anything. He seems to be falling asleep again. We dump him in the backseat, and then Audrey climbs in back too.

"Which way?" asks Jin-Ae.

Audrey rolls down her window, and lights a cigarette. Eyes closed, Frank doesn't notice. I turn on the computer and find a campground in Lehigh Gorge State Park, about fifty minutes away.

March 11

Frank: my father is so demanding and i can't do anything right
Jin-Ae: my family is like that . . . high pressure
Audrey: at least your dad wants something for u. mine
  left when i was 2. i never hear from him, ever. he's
  in jail now, in florida. not like he doesn't have time
  to write

Owen: *my dad left three years ago. had an affair. i don't hear*
   from him either
Audrey: *is that y u tried to kill yourself?*
Owen: *idk*

BY THE TIME WE PULL INTO THE CAMPGROUND, FRANK IS asleep. We leave him in the car, and set up the tent. I don't change my shirt. I like how it looks, all bloody and red on my chest. When I try to touch my nose, it stings.

"I wonder if football camp was everything he wanted?" Audrey asks, sounding remarkably soft.

"Good question." Jin-Ae grabs a citronella candle and lights it. "Hate bugs. Maybe he just wanted to get trashed."

For the first time, I notice Audrey's freckles. Maybe the sun brought them out. The top of her head is red, her frying pan scar, a deeper purple. Surprisingly I want to kiss her on the head. The three of us bring out all the food from the trunk and randomly start eating, no organized meal, Pop-Tarts again, crackers and cheese, whatever we grab.

"We should probably eat better," Jin-Ae says. "Cook a meal once in a while."

"No stove," Audrey says. "We could stop at a diner, though."

"I could eat a meal," I say.

"I'm going to go get some stuff," says Jin-Ae. "A little stove, mess kit."

"I'm a vegetarian," says Audrey. I'm surprised by this fact. "So get macaroni and cheese."

Jin-Ae tilts her head. "For how long?"

"A long time. First grade, I think. I hate how they kill the animals."

I expect more from Jin-Ae, but she doesn't say anything about it. Instead she asks, "Ride or stay here?"

Audrey answers for us both. "Me and Owen will stay here and make a fire."

March 19

Frank: how serious of a suicide attempt did u make w/pills, Owen?

Owen: y do u ask?

Frank: b/c i think i really almost died. i wanted to know if anyone else did too

Owen: i had to eat charcoal like u

Frank: did u need medical treatment to stay alive?

Owen: i took aspirin and coca-cola. that was stupid

Frank: would that kill you if u didn't get your stomach pumped?

Owen: idk

Frank: i would have died they said

Frank: i drank a lot of whiskey and took tylenol and percocets

*Owen: most times i've tried nothing happened with the
hospital*

Frank: like what?

*Owen: i tried to drown myself. went to the psych hospital
not the regular hospital*

Frank: i only tried once, a long time ago

Owen: once is all it takes for some people

I HAVE NEVER BEEN ALONE WITH AUDREY BEFORE. WE'VE
chatted online alone, but otherwise we're always in a group. I
feel funny, nervous. The campground is very wooded, with a
hill leading down to a river behind our tent. We can hear the
water, far away. Getting late, the sun heads lower toward the
trees. Darkness always comes.

Audrey walks off, looking for wood. I follow. From behind,
I see how much like a girl she looks, swishier than a boy, curvy.
As she turns around to glance at me, I change my look, embarrassed that she's caught me watching her butt. She doesn't seem
to notice.

That night, Frank never wakes up, even though we have
a fire and stay up until about eleven o'clock. Jin-Ae sleeps in
the front seat with Frank in the back of the car. Audrey and
I share the tent. She makes me leave my bloody shirt in the
trunk, in case the blood will bring a bear or ants or anything

wild. All night I keep opening my eyes, waking up to look at her in the pitch-black darkness. I feel all tight and nervous, stiff, like I should be careful how I move, not to touch her or brush against her. Audrey is a very sound sleeper who keeps her mouth open, and lies on her side. I don't sleep too well, not too deep, and I'm up for good as soon as the tent starts to turn gray instead of being dark. I can see her freckles, more still than yesterday, although her head doesn't look as pink and sunburned. When I lean close, I can smell her breath. I find myself leaning in closer, a lot, so I can smell her. I don't know if I have ever been so close to someone else's face for so long.

Only I'm wrong, I suppose. Maybe not for so long. But I remember his face. So clear. His face will never go away.

I have never written a suicide note before, even though I have tried to kill myself a lot. I'll tell you why I try to kill myself. I'm a murderer.

March 30

Jin-Ae: i think u are the only one in therapy owen

Owen: didn't hastings tell u to go to a counselor too?

Jin-Ae: yes but my family doesn't believe in it

Audrey: they should

Frank: my family was supposed to get me a counselor after i tried, but they never did

Jin-Ae: how old were u the first time u tried to kill yourself?

Frank: only time — 13

Owen: 7

Jin-Ae: SEVEN?!!

Audrey: 7 7 7???

Owen: i ran into traffic so i could die and be with my brother in heaven. my parents didn't let me go to his funeral

I'm used to all of the questions that people ask you when you try to kill yourself, mostly from the professional people. One of the main things they do is try to get you to think about the consequences. I've been asked by lots of people, "What happens if you do kill yourself?" They want to know about what it would be like for other people around you, like the person who would find your body, the other kids at school, whoever would have to clean up the blood, what your family holidays would be like.

Some of that I know about because of when my brother Forrest died. My mother found his body, floating in the pool. She screamed and cried and called 911. I thought she would never stop calling his name. When someone in your family dies young, I think it is very similar to suicide. My father made a company empty the entire pool to make sure that there was no blood anywhere. And my brother James was the only one who would go into the pool for weeks after Forrest died. Later, when we moved to New Jersey, I was very surprised when our new house had a pool.

When you attempt suicide, the counselors try to talk you out of trying it again by asking you about other people, which is good prevention if you care about other people. Seeing as my dad left, I don't care about him much. My brother James does his own thing, since he's away at college. Technically, James is home for the summer, but he's not really there, just working at a camp. And my mother is so depressed that she doesn't care what happens to me, not the way she should. I mean, she does, but mainly because I'm something else that she can't handle, and wants to be different. She told my therapist, Sherri, that I was never the same after Forrest died. Really, my mom was never the same. And then when my dad left, she became a mess. She has to go to therapy herself now, and she takes antidepressants, which they have tried to give to me but I don't take. Sometimes I feel like the parent, and that isn't fair. There's nobody left to take care of me. My father is gone, my brother has his own life in college, and my mother is incompetent. So I don't really need anybody, anyway. And when Sherri asks questions about who would find me if I killed myself and what their reaction would be, I think that whoever knew me would be sad. But then everybody would get over it. I would fade away. I don't think I'm that important to anyone. Nobody's opinion about me killing myself would stop me from doing it.

That was what happened the time I tried to kill myself by drowning. I didn't care who would find me. I remember it was my fourteenth birthday, the same age as Forrest when he died. I put on three pairs of pants and my hiking boots, and also three shirts and my winter coat. It was awkward, but I took all of the big stones from the garden and loaded up every single pocket in each pair of pants and the coat. I felt so heavy walking, like I could barely move. Nobody was home. My mother was at her friend's house, and James stayed after school to play baseball again. I loaded all the cans of soup and beans and vegetables and everything we had in the cabinets into my backpack, and put that on, too. I must have had a hundred pounds of stuff on me. I didn't leave a note. I just walked over to the edge of the pool and looked at the water. The pool had only been open a couple of days for the summer season, and I could see dirt still in the bottom from the winter. I kept thinking about Forrest. That's when I jumped in. I stepped in, really, because I was wearing too much weight to jump. I sank like a rock. The pool is only eight feet deep at the deep end. After a few seconds I could feel my feet at the bottom.

Drowning is not as peaceful as you might think. Your body does not want to breathe in water. Even with all of those rocks and cans and me jumping in on purpose to try to kill myself, my body was fighting. I found that very strange. Like, somewhere inside there's a part that doesn't want to die, no matter what. I opened my mouth to swallow and breathe the water, but nothing would happen. As if some other part was in control. I could feel the pressure in my head building up and I was saying, inside, "Please, please, please." I don't know what I was asking for. Finally, I bent my knees and pushed off of the bottom. My head burst out of the water, and I swallowed a big gulp of air before I went down again. The second time I went under, I could tell it wouldn't work to drown myself, so I took off my backpack and let it go. Then I came up for air again, which was so much easier without the backpack. I swam to the edge and wanted to climb out, but all of the clothes and rocks were too heavy. I took off everything except my underwear and let it all sink to the bottom, even my boots. When I finally climbed out, I stared down at all the stuff and wondered if that's what I would have looked like if I had sunk instead of come up for air.

Later, James found all of my things in the bottom of the pool. I wanted to lie, but I couldn't think of a good one. I told him that I tried to drown myself. At first he didn't believe me, then he told our mother. I think that was the first time she tried to call my father since he'd left. He wouldn't talk to her. She took me to the hospital instead. That was the first time someone asked me who would find my dead body. That was the first time I realized I didn't care.

They say that if you really want to kill yourself, no one can stop you. There are too many ways to do it. You can jump off a bridge or a building. You can hang yourself. You can crash a car or slit your wrists or swim out really far into the ocean until you drown. Sometimes I wonder why I'm not dead, if I really wanted to kill myself. One of the therapists at Hastings, maybe it was an orderly, said I might be doing it for attention. He's probably right. Of course I could use attention. Who couldn't? But what kind of attention and from who? Sometimes I think maybe from my father, my dear old daddy, who never calls, not even when his son tried to drown himself. He, I don't understand, just moved away. I think my mother was too much for him to handle. She probably didn't have sex with him anymore. I think it's weird to think of your parents having sex, but weirder to think that they stopped having it. My guess is that my mother didn't have sex with my dad after Forrest drowned. And she's always crying and meddling in my business and not a lot of fun to be around in any way. She wants everything organized, like the house has to be crazy-spotless clean. Worse, even after my father is gone for almost three years now, she still has this painted birdhouse with both of their names on it right in the front stairway. I wish she would get rid of it.

I LAY THERE, WATCHING AUDREY SLEEP. SHE SMELLS GOOD, sweet. I notice her scar is about eight inches long, across the top of her head and down to her ear. Then I watch her wake up, kind of slow. She moves her arms first and then her face a little bit at a time. I have never watched someone wake up like that before. She looks beautiful. Audrey, maybe I will tell you someday.

Top Ten Athletes Frank Said Should Kill Themselves

10. Mitch Williams, Phillies pitcher, gave up the 1993 World Series–ending walk-off home run

9. Bobby Riggs, Wimbledon men's tennis champ, lost tennis game to Billie Jean King (a woman)

8. Mike Tyson, heavyweight champ, became rapist and cannibal

7. Terrell Owens, football jerk

6. O. J. Simpson, football murderer who got away with it

5. Shoeless Joe Jackson, White Sox left fielder, purposefully lost the 1919 World Series

4. Michael Vick, quarterback, dog killer

3. Barry Bonds, home-run hitter, steroid freak

2. Scott Norwood, Buffalo Bills kicker, missed and lost Super Bowl XXV

1. Bill Buckner, Red Sox first baseman, blew the 1986 World Series, ground ball rolled between his legs

Rain arrives at about seven o'clock. Audrey and I are still in the tent. I hear the first raindrops, then a pretty steady drumming. Jin-Ae curses loud enough for me to hear her. She's complaining about an open window in the car.

I walk over. Frank looks and smells hungover. He needs a shower. They rearrange themselves, and I climb into the car. We don't talk; maybe Frank's head hurts too much.

Jin-Ae starts to sharpen her nails, and I do mean sharpen. Not like most girls do with nail polish and a manicure. She files them into a point. I think that's one of the ways she cuts herself, if she doesn't have a knife or a razor or a pin. They look like claws. "Let's figure out how to keep our parents off our backs," she says.

"Why?" Audrey asks, appearing at the door.

"Well, cops for one. Aren't you the runaway?"

"Touché," says Audrey. Then she takes off toward the showers, screaming "Runaway!"

"Just call," says Frank, shaking his head slowly.

Jin-Ae opens the phone and dials, leaves a message on the answering machine. I laugh when I hear her say that she'll buy her mother a Lehigh bumper sticker.

Later, we drive to the campus and walk around, looking at the buildings. Mainly the place is empty because, according to Frank, it's summer session. Jin-Ae wants to e-mail her mother.

Everybody writes something to their family. Basically, "Hello. I am fine."

The last thing I do is post my journal, knowing that none of them will see it. When everything is done, anybody who wants can read it.

April 2

Owen: *lots of famous people kill themselves. hitler,*
judas, nero

Jin-Ae: *sylvia plath*

Audrey: *KURT COBAIN—hello. duh. Nirvana*

Jin-Ae: *anne sexton*

Audrey: *kurt cobain. did u hear me?*

Frank: *lots of them were also crazy*

Jin-Ae: *yes we heard. and?*

Audrey: *the BEST EVER*

Jin-Ae: *yeah, u talk about them so much it gets on my*
NIRVES-ana

Audrey: *i know everything about nirvana, grunge, seattle.*
everything. maybe i was born too late

Jin-Ae: *and in new jersey*

Audrey: *lol*

Frank: *lmfao*

Audrey: *i'm dying to go to seattle*

I know it's stupid and that I have said it before, but I wonder what it feels like to die.

I've read more on psychology than most teenagers. Mainly this is because I find it interesting and because I have talked to so many social workers and counselors. I think I would be a good counselor myself. I know what things mean, about self-esteem and trying to like yourself.

I always thought the school counselor, Mr. Clark, was the smartest when it came to that last one, even though no one is really supposed to think the school counselor is more than a dull man in a tie. Once, when the school nurse asked me about taking pills, she brought him in because I think she was tired of trying to figure out how to deal with me. He said something I remember very clearly. "Self-esteem is overrated. Anyone will think they color great if enough people tell them. Artificial praise. Down inside, compliments like that are hollow."

I remember that so well, because he was the first one who made sense. My mother took me to a counselor in first grade, when I was seven, after Forrest died. That therapist—I don't even remember what he looked like—told her that I needed better self-esteem. I never knew what that meant, even though she would say it to me and my father and the rest of my family. I always thought I liked myself well enough.

Mr. Clark said, "Real self-worth comes from mastery,

from getting good at something. It doesn't matter what. Then you don't have to worry about empty compliments. You don't worry about what other people think. You have self-respect."

I remember him standing up, and having the bottom button of his shirt open. I saw his belly button. I remember thinking he had self-respect, because he didn't care if I saw his stomach.

The only things I'm really good at are reading, and, I suppose, I'm becoming an expert at suicide nowadays, which is probably not too good unless I'm helping other people. That's funny, in a way, because I have noticed so many people talking about killing themselves that Mr. Clark told me I should have an office in school. (That was a joke.) He said I gave him more referrals than anyone else in the whole school, including teachers and the school's police officer combined.

I can tell you all of the things that they have said about me, all of the right words and clinical diagnoses that I have read about me, or so they say, in the DSM, the doctor's book of crazies. They say I have an anxiety disorder, separation anxiety, bipolarity, low self-esteem, suicidal tendencies, poor social-ization, poor communication, maladaptive coping mecha-nism, post-traumatic stress disorder, delayed grief reaction, overcompensation for guilt and remorse, overly active nervous system, disturbances of thoughts and emotions, family problems, and histrionic overreactions. They also said things I'm not: obsessive-compulsive, drug addicted, violent toward others, overachieving, anorexic, bulimic, homicidal, homosexual, conduct disorder, ADD, dyslexic, and autistic.

I only understand half of that stuff, but I know what it means. Basically, I'm screwed.

BACK ON THE ROAD. MY NOSE IS STILL SORE. MAYBE FRANK BROKE it. We have a lot of miles to go. Our plan is to travel at least nine hours a day, more if we can, so that we can be in Colorado on June 30, for Hunter S. Thompson, my celebrity. That's three days from now. No one says we must keep that schedule, but I think we all want to be there anyway, in order to be at Hemingway's grave on his death day anniversary. Frank called his brother, but he wasn't home. Me and Audrey didn't call.

We're on the Pennsylvania Turnpike now, then we'll go through Ohio, Indiana, Illinois, Iowa, and keep going straight until the Rocky Mountains show up. Frank isn't hung over anymore. At least I don't think so. He doesn't look as bad. Audrey took a shower and for the first time, wore a shirt without long sleeves. It was a Nirvana T-shirt with a happy face on the front. No surprise there. Jin-Ae painted her fingernails with Audrey's purple nail polish, which, according to her, is completely out of character. She said that she never paints her nails at all.

April 4

Jin-Ae: r u suicidal or not?

Audrey: i did try so i guess yes

Frank: i'm confused by all of this

Jin-Ae: u must be a very good liar

Audrey: i grew up that way. i always had to make up
  stories. this was no different

Jin-Ae: i thought u jumped off the roof?

Audrey: yes

Jin-Ae: and?

Audrey: AND then i said it was an accident to my family.
  told them i was sunbathing up there

Jin-Ae: in march?

Audrey: my boyfriend, ryan, dumped me for someone else.
  i was mad

Jin-Ae: u have to be pretty mad to jump off of a roof

Audrey: i don't think i wanted to die. its just . . . idk . . .
  u have to be pretty mad to do any of the stuff i did.
  or u guys. mad angry or mad crazy.

Frank: probably both

Audrey: both my legs are broken

Frank: now?

Audrey: still in a wheelchair. until may they say

Frank pulls in at one of the rest stops on the highway. "Pit stop," he says.

"What state are we in?" asks Jin-Ae.

"Confused," Audrey answers.

"Still Pennsylvania," Frank says. "Maybe an hour until Ohio."

I push trash with my feet. We have been living in the car, mostly, for days now. Three soda cans are at my feet, plus Pop-Tarts wrappers, licorice, and crumbs; a bunch of junk. Still in the backseat, I start to collect some of the trash.

"Go, go, go!" shouts Audrey, practically pushing Jin-Ae out of the car. "I gotta go."

"Me too," says Jin-Ae. They race off toward the restrooms. Frank starts toward the men's room, sees that I'm collecting garbage, and then slows.

"Go ahead," I say. "I'll do the rest."

He does.

I straighten the car, making more room for myself. One of the blankets in the backseat needs to be untangled, because Audrey and I have pushed it into a ball. Several CDs are out of their cases and on the floor where Jin-Ae sits in the front. Audrey's pink socks lay in the back window, along with Frank's hat and a jacket. I grab Audrey's black shirt, which is crumpled in a ball. I smell her as I lift it. My pillow is crammed behind Frank's seat. I grab the pillow and toss it on top of Audrey's socks, out of the way. As I reach under Frank's seat, looking for money or trash, I grab something metallic and hard.

Frank has brought a gun.

I've never touched one before. Not a real one. I'm surprised how heavy it feels.

I look up, suddenly scared. Police? Frank? The girls? No one is around. I hold the gun low, below the window, so that anyone walking by won't see me with a pistol.

I think the gun is a .38. I don't know for sure. I know it's not an automatic or a semiautomatic because of the spinner. I forget what that part is called. I do know there is no clip, which means it holds six bullets. A six-shooter. The handle is black, the barrel is black, and the hammer is black. I could guess it weighs six pounds, only I know it doesn't—not that heavy I'm sure.

I can feel my face hot and flush and full of adrenaline. *Frank brought a gun!*

This is serious, like he-really-means-to-kill-himself serious, seal-the-deal serious. Serious, like maybe-he-means-to-kill-us serious. My hands start to tremble.

A .22 is smaller, I think. And a .45, a .45 magnum, is bigger, longer. I wonder if it's Frank's gun. Probably his father's. Probably stolen from his father who's out of the country and doesn't even know it's gone.

I put my finger on the trigger. If I wanted to, I could kill myself right now. Shoot myself in the backseat and never have to try again, be done with it. I remember the right way to put the gun in my mouth and point it upward toward the back. Maybe I could do it now, lift the gun, point, and pull.

I stare at the black shape. I start to raise the gun up. I remember my promise. To die at the end. That means I have to live now.

Suddenly I'm crying. Bad. Hard. My legs shake. My breath quavers. I drop the gun on the floor and grab for my pillow, close my eyes.

I don't know if I want to die. I just want to be happy. I want to feel better.

For what feels like a long time, I hold the pillow to my chest and keep crying. I don't care what anyone thinks. I don't care. When I open my eyes, I see that I'm also holding one of Audrey's socks, right up close to my throat. Something about that feels so good. I let out a sigh.

The others will be back soon. With my foot, I slide the gun back under Frank's seat to its hiding place. I'll have to think about whether or not to tell the girls. I wonder what I would say to them or Frank.

Then I scoop up the trash and head toward the bathroom. I have to pee, and I need a drink.

April 8

Frank: whats your preferred way to die everybody?

82 * albert borris

Jin-Ae: that's a really good question, Frank

Frank: thanks

Jin-Ae: no, i mean it. i have to think about it. anyone? do u know frank?

Frank: i think i want something sure. not like the pills

Jin-Ae: u mean like when your family found you?

Frank. i think i'd like to die in my sleep so it wouldn't hurt, but . . .

Frank: if i did kill myself i would shoot myself. out in the woods someplace where it wouldn't be messy like in a house or anything

Audrey: that's considerate of u

Jin-Ae: smart-ass

Frank: something quick

Jin-Ae: i think i'd want the opposite. something to enjoy

Audrey: enjoy?

Jin-Ae: i know it sounds crazy, but slow, like a bath and the blood coming out of my wrists slow, soft

Audrey: candles and music, right?

Jin-Ae: and a glass of wine—spiked with ecstacy

Audrey: oh the drama!! gee. interesting. owen?

Owen: i'm still thinking

Frank: i wouldn't want anyone to stop me, and i want to make sure that i couldn't change my mind—like the bathtub i could

Jin-Ae: i wouldn't change my mind

Audrey: i think i would like to jump off of a huge cliff into the ocean

Audrey: i mean huge, like where i was flying, five hundred feet. maybe jump out of a plane, but not over land, into the ocean

Owen: i would like to be transported . . . i mean like a transporter beam out into space

Owen: i'd like all of my molecules to be beamed out into the emptiness of space so that there was no trace of me at all, anywhere. i'd be everywhere all at once

Jin-Ae: u know that's not real, owen

Owen: i don't care. u asked how i wanted to die. that would be what i would like

Audrey: luv it owen, u freak!

THEY ARE ALL WAITING FOR ME AT THE CAR WHEN I RETURN. Frank and Jin-Ae hold soda cans. Audrey smokes a cigarette. "Frank has a new plan," Audrey says. "We're going to Chicago."

Jin-Ae's face looks pained.

"Actually," says Frank, "we're going to stop at Wrigley Field to see the Cubs."

"Why?" I ask.

"Because I want to. It's on my death list. Jin-Ae started it."

Jin-Ae sighs loudly. She tips back her soda and finishes it. Then shakes her head. "I didn't . . ." Her voice trails off.

Frank pulls out a piece of paper from his back pocket. "Here, see. I made a list. Jin-Ae asked what we wanted to do before we died. I came up with ten things." He waves the paper in front of me, as though I can read it. "Wrigley Field, number one. It's on the way."

"I'm not going," says Jin-Ae.

"Me either," says Audrey. "Football camp. Baseball. Too much testosterone."

"Crap."

"No. You go," says Audrey. "We'll do something in Chicago. Owen will go with you."

Frank looks at me. I nod.

Audrey stubs out her cigarette. "Long ride. Let's get started. And give me that list." She snatches it from Frank. "I want to know what else we're in for."

Frank doesn't object. As we climb into the car Audrey starts to read aloud. "He wasn't kidding, number one: Go to Wrigley Field to see a Cubs game."

Doors slam. As Frank starts the engine, he says, "Don't do that. Don't read it like that. That's wrong."

"Why? You're making us go to Chicago."

"It's on the way."

"I want to know what else we'll be doing," Audrey says firmly.

"Fine," says Frank. "Then you are all going to do lists too. And read them out loud."

"Fine."

He shifts into drive. "Fine." The wheels screech as we zoom out of the parking lot. Jin-Ae shakes her head. I close my eyes to pretend to sleep. Audrey continues reading Frank's list out loud.

"Number two: Write for *Sports Illustrated*. Interesting. Number three: Broadcast a championship basketball game. You're sort of a jock, Frank." She smiles.

Frank doesn't reply.

"Start writing, boy," chimes in Jin-Ae. "Death Valley awaits."

"Oh." Audrey chuckles. "Looks like your comment inspired him, Jin-Ae. Number four: Have sex, any kind."

"Whoa," says Jin-Ae.

Frank looks embarrassed. "Oh, I forgot I put that on there."

"That's kind of sweet," Audrey says. "Number five: Meet Lance Armstrong. Number six: Tell my father he is wrong about life. I like that, Frank. I'd do something like that too. Number seven: Visit Hemingway's grave. Good, we already plan to do that. But oh, what about this?"

We're back at full speed on the highway. I pull the blanket up over me and lean to the side. I need a nap, tired from crying.

"Number eight: Hike to the South Pole? We can't drive there, Frank."

"I know. Remind me one more time how I'm a failure. It's just something I want to do."

"Before you die?" asks Jin-Ae. "What about our deal that—"

"Shush," Audrey says. Jin-Ae stops. "Number nine: Get a Hummer. The car, right? Not number four for a second time, correct?"

Frank squirms. No comment.

"Number ten: Sing the national anthem at a pro-football game? What the heck, Frank?"

Jin-Ae intercedes. "Give him a break, Audrey. He can wish, it just won't happen in this life. Besides, I'd like to hear your list."

"You will," says Frank.

Audrey starts to say something about adding number eleven, but I can't keep myself awake enough to listen.

April 9

Audrey: wat do u want on your gravestone
Jin-Ae: we did that in the hospital
Owen: no. the counselors made us write our obituary, and
    pretend that someone in our family had to write it
Jin-Ae: thank u mr. technicality
Frank: gone but not forgotten

Jin-Ae: gravestone? name & date

Audrey: nuthin else? loving daughter?

Jin-Ae: haha

Audrey: i'd like mine to say queen of the universe

Jin-Ae: nice. owen?

Owen: nothing. well maybe just good-bye

WHEN I WAKE UP, THE SUN IS RISING. JIN-AE IS DRIVING. THE first thing I think of is Frank's gun. I wonder if it's still under the seat. Are there bullets in the gun? Was I really thinking of shooting myself yesterday?

At Hastings there were lots of kids who were suicidal. One kid said he put a gun in his mouth. And one of the kids who killed themselves in Cherry Hill had shot himself. I think he did, at least. They don't tell you much about kids who kill themselves. At school they try to not make a big deal out of it, even though lots of the kids freak out. I didn't cry when I found out about the last one, a college freshman who graduated from my high school last year. Mostly the juniors and seniors were upset. I know how the counselors work, what they look for. I even read the crisis manual for the high school. Mr. Clark, the school counselor, let me borrow it, which I thought was kind of funny. He told me that I knew so much about suicide, I might as well tell him what I thought about how the school handled things. They call parents and make teachers or counselors go into the classroom to tell the students what's happened. No assemblies, the book says, to prevent mass hysteria. They never tell you the details of how a kid died either, like if he hung himself or shot himself. You have to look in the papers. And, to quote the manual, "Do nothing that will glorify suicide." So they don't plant trees or name hallways after the kids who kill themselves. Nothing to make more kids want to kill themselves. If you ask me, any kid who wants to kill themselves so that a hallway in their high school can be named after them is truly messed up. They will probably kill themselves no matter what the school does or doesn't do.

They always look out for the troubled kids right after a suicide. I guess that means I'm troubled. Kids who have tried to kill themselves before, or kids who knew the dead ones. They try to talk to kids who have dead parents or who are crazy. I think they don't want everyone killing themselves at the same time.

I guess it was kind of nice of Mr. Clark to lend me that book and ask my opinion, even though I didn't have much to say. I thought they should have a hotline for kids to call in case they felt suicidal. He liked that idea, too.

I wonder what Mr. Clark would think about Frank's gun, about me picking it up. Scared, probably.

"I think I'm going to go to hell," Jin-Ae says. I know

she's talking to me. Frank and Audrey haven't moved, still sleeping. I yawn and sit up in the backseat. "Morning, sleepy head." She smiles.

I mumble something as I yawn again.

"You slept for hours, Owen. And you snore. We stopped three times, and you never stirred. I thought you might have been dead, but Audrey checked your pulse and breathing—"

"Where are we?" I interrupt.

"An hour from Indianapolis."

Jin-Ae, from what I can see of her in the mirror, looks both tired and awake. Coffee probably, the way she's rambling. "We tried to stop at the James Dean Museum. You didn't wake up at all."

"Bathroom?" I ask.

"Next exit, okay? Anyway, he didn't suicide and the place was closed years ago."

I nod, noticing the way she uses "suicide" like a verb. An action. I look down to where my feet go under the seat and where the gun is hidden. Audrey's pink socks, now back on her feet, rest there.

Jin-Ae rambles. "I used your computer, Owen. Hope you don't mind."

"What did you find?"

"Directions, mostly. And baseball stuff. The game starts

at seven, so we'll be there in plenty of time. Audrey and I are going to the gay community center."

"Bingo?"

"Nope. Teen night. I'm going to convert Audrey to gay by making her go."

I spot a sign for the next exit. Two miles. I think I can last that long.

She keeps talking. "I'm already going to hell, because I lie so much to my parents. And they are so anti-gay. I'm going to rot and burn forever."

"This is hell," says Audrey. She speaks, wakes without moving a muscle. "People rambling on and waking me up."

"Sorry," I whisper.

"Actually, I don't believe in hell," says Audrey. "Or God." She moves, turning so that her legs rest across my lap. I like the position, feels comfortable. "You okay driving?"

"Fine. Frank went out about an hour ago. I slept most of the night."

A state trooper pulls up on our left. Audrey stiffens, slinks lower in the seat. Ahead, the exit sign looms. "Nuts," Audrey whispers, sinking even lower. I wonder why she's trying to hide, why she—

"Be cool," Jin-Ae says calmly, still looking straight ahead. "Thought your mom wouldn't care."

Audrey grunts. Jin-Ae keeps watching the road, not the cop.

Finally the exit arrives. The trooper stays on the expressway. We pull into some small gas station and breakfast joint. We leave Frank in the car, sleeping, and head to the bathrooms.

I FIND THIS LIST JIN-AE AND AUDREY MADE ON THE COMPUTER while I was sleeping:

Top Ten Weird Celebrity Death Sites

10. Graceland, Elvis, overdose on the toilet
9. European castle where Alexander the Great drank himself to death
8. Butchery in England where Sir Arthur Aston was beat to death with his own wooden leg
7. Dallas library, John F. Kennedy shot
6. Pyramids in Egypt, Cleopatra's suicide by snakebites
5. Paris, tunnel where Princess Diana's car crashed
4. London, apartment where both Keith Moon overdosed and Mama Cass choked to death on a ham sandwich
3. Old Giant Stadium end zone, Jimmy Hoffa buried in concrete?
2. Belmont Park racetrack, Frank Hayes won the 1923 race while dead
1. Paris, bathtub where Jim Morrison died of mysterious circumstances

April 10

Owen: i found a website of famous suicide people for our
     club

Audrey: y? forget it. u r strange. what does it say about kurt?

Owen: that he killed himself with a shotgun. he was a heroin
     addict

Audrey: some people think courtney love killed him. murder
     not suicide

Owen: u think that?

Audrey: no. that theory is for people who can't deal with the
     truth

Jin-Ae: is there something on a porn actress called
     savannah?

Owen: wait, i'll look

Audrey: a porn actress?

Jin-Ae: she was very famous. dated all these rock stars.
     greg allman, vince neil of motley crew, slash of guns n
     roses, billy idol, axl rose, marky mark

Audrey: how do u know all this? and i wouldn't call them all
     famous

Jin-Ae: i have some of her videos

Audrey: porn videos!? i thought u were a good kid

Jin-Ae: it was an accident, i think. my parents bought me
     some videos on ebay, a history collection. there were
     three of her videos in there. they are old, from the

90s. i think someone was playing a joke

Owen: there's a page on her. her real name is shannon wilsey,

    shot herself on July 11, 1994. she crashed her car first

Jin-Ae: most girls probably don't watch porn. i have never

    told anyone before. she made me a lesbian

Audrey: u have a girlfriend?

Jin-Ae: no

Audrey: ever?

Jin-Ae: not really

Audrey: she killed herself?

Jin-Ae: yes

Audrey: she probably made u suicidal not lesbian

"Can't we tell Frank we stopped at the stadium and he didn't wake up?" Jin-Ae asks. "Too hung over?"

Audrey shakes her head.

The Colts' stadium comes into view. Jin-Ae takes the exit ramp too fast. The wheels squeal. Then we hit the warning bumps on the side of the road, the kind that make that rattling noise. She jams the brakes. Nothing bad happens. Frank stirs but doesn't wake.

"There's not even a grave—"

"Jin-Ae," Audrey interrupts harshly. Jin-Ae stops talking. Apparently the three of them decided to add this arena to the trip while I was sleeping. Or maybe just Frank and Audrey agreed. Jin-Ae isn't happy. When we make our way into the parking lot, Jin-Ae nudges Frank awake. He rouses himself slowly as Jin-Ae stops the car.

"Well?" Audrey asks. No one answers.

The stadium looks deserted. A few cars line the parking lot. I don't see anyone. Stiffly we climb out.

"This is stupid. He didn't hang himself here," says Jin-Ae.

Frank opens the trunk. He grabs his football and a few other things I can't make out.

"James Dungy was the son of Tony Dungy, coach of the Colts," Frank explains. "He killed himself in Florida. Tied his belt to a ceiling fan. His dad coached here."

"Doesn't count. Not a celebrity," says Jin-Ae, slamming the trunk shut. "Not his gravesite."

Frank shrugs. He walks off toward the stadium. Jin-Ae moans, then runs off right next to him.

I pause, waiting to see what Audrey will do. She slaps the trunk with an open hand a few times. "Ooh, it's so not fair, Owen," she whines, mocking Jin-Ae.

Then she grabs me by the arm, leading me toward the other two. We catch them before they reach the stadium gates, which are locked. Frank turns his head around, like he's looking for someone. Very deliberately, he walks away from the gates. He pauses next to a metal sign that reads TICKET HOLDERS ONLY.

Frank pulls out a Sharpie. He scrawls "RIP James Dungy—

from the Suicide Dogs" in small black letters on the sign, just below the words.

"Wait," I say. I don't tell them why, but I run over to a small tree. I dig up a stone about the size of a quarter. When I get back, I take the marker from Frank and write "RIP James" on the rock, and place it next to the sign.

"Gravestone," I whisper.

Audrey exhales loudly.

Suddenly Frank punts the football over the gate. He shouts "James" really loud. The ball drops with a thud. We hear it roll, then silence.

"He killed himself when the Colts were 13–0," Frank says to us. "Perfect season. No wonder. Can't live up to that."

None of us say anything. Even the stadium is quiet. Like a dead person. All those visitors during football season, cheering, now nothing. I suppose everything dies, even football games.

Finally Audrey says, "Let's get breakfast."

"Can we actually sit down in a diner or something?" asks Jin-Ae.

"For you," Audrey answers, smiling too big, "anything."

The girls head toward the car. Frank and me hold the bars and stare through the gates for a long time.

April 16

Frank: my dad wants me to play football at college

Jin-Ae: and?

Frank: i'll be in 12th grade and i never played in a game.

  i'm more likely to grow another head

Audrey: that'd be intersting

Frank:. i'm a loser. lost a wrestling match to a girl

Audrey: u tried to kill yourself because u lost to a girl?

Frank: no. i lost in 9th grade. i tried to kill myself like 7th grade

Audrey: so what if u lost?

Frank: that's not all. if u ever see me, i'm ugly. pimples and

  nothing but arms and legs. my body's too short.

  uncoordinated

Audrey: that all?

Frank: no . . . u ever know that u weren't good enuf. i mean

  really know it?

Audrey: every day

Frank: most days i don't remember to brush my teeth or my

  hair

Audrey: gross

Frank: i came in last in the 50 yard dash in 5th grade. last.

  even the fat kid beat me

CHICAGO. POPULATION: FOUR MILLION? I DON'T KNOW. I DIDN'T
look it up. I just guessed. I know it's bigger than Philadelphia
and smaller than New York City. I'd never been before today.
What do I know about it? Windy. Really cold in the winter.

On the Great Lakes. The Sears Tower is the tallest building there, and some French or Australian guy climbed it once, without gear. Chicago Cubs. Michael Jordan. I know a little more about baseball, because of my brother James who plays in college. The White Sox won the World Series in 2000 something. The Cubs never win. Sammy Sosa was a Cub, but he was traded. Wrigley Field is one of the oldest and most famous stadiums. Only day games used to be played there, but they added lights in the eighties.

Frank and I drop the girls off downtown. Jin-Ae says, "Call us after the game."

Frank and me get to the baseball field around four o'clock. The game doesn't start until seven. Here is the amazing part: Frank calls the stadium.

He says, "I want to interview the broadcaster for the Diamondbacks." He lies! It is incredible. He makes up a whole story. I am from Arizona, and doing a report for school. I don't understand it all, but Frank ends up talking to the broadcaster on the phone. The guy isn't at the stadium, but at his hotel, arriving soon.

We walk around to the players' entrance and wait.

Quite a few people go in and out until a white-haired man waves us over. Frank knows him right away. I haven't ever met someone famous. We shake hands, and Frank begins talking and talking.

"How long have you been broadcasting?" Frank starts.

I walk behind him and Whitey as we head inside. We don't have tickets, but we go in anyway.

"Where was your first job?"

I haven't ever been in the back part of a stadium. As far as games go, I've watched a lot of baseball, because my mother drags me along to James's games.

"Do you think if you aren't a former player you can get a job in broadcasting?"

From behind, they look like a dad and kid going to a game, talking about the team. Whitey even puts his hand on Frank's shoulder.

Frank turns to me. "Hear that?"

"What?" I reply.

"We can watch the game from the announcers' booth."

Frank is thrilled. I am bored.

We walk around the stadium and visit the locker rooms with Whitey. He gives us passes, so that we can meet him in the booth later. Then Frank leads me toward seats near the dugout, fourth row, behind third base.

"Batting practice," he says.

Frank buys a beer at the food stand. Then we sit while both teams warm up. I look through the suicide Web site.

"Frank," I say. "I found a baseball player suicide."

"Who?" Frank asks loudly.

"Donnie Moore."

"Vague recollection."

"Pitcher for the Angels. Says he lost a big game to the Red Sox in 1986."

"Right," Frank says, tossing his empty beer cup to the ground.

"He shot himself," I add, wondering if Frank will say anything about his gun.

He doesn't. "Where?"

"Head."

Frank sighs. "I mean, where on the planet."

I keep reading, then say, "Anaheim."

"Too far. We don't need another one, anyway," Frank replies.

Later, just before we enter the announcer's booth, Frank buys another beer. That gets me thinking, he better not get drunk.

We have to sit in folding chairs against the back wall. Whitey waves us in, then leans forward into a microphone to talk. The announcers talk all the time, since it's radio. One guy smokes, which surprises me.

"Frank," I whisper, so that the announcers don't hear. "What if they catch you drinking?"

"They won't."

"Arrested. End of the trip," I say. He doesn't reply. I take the beer from his hand and pretend to take a sip.

"Help yourself," Frank says sarcastically.

I shrug. Then I stand up and walk into the bathroom, cup in hand. I don't really have to go. Instead I dump about half the liquid in the sink. In the mirror, my nose looks purplish from Frank's accidental punch. Returning, I give Frank back a much smaller beer. He looks at me, at the cup, says nothing.

A few innings later, Frank buys another beer. "I think maybe," he says, "I could play baseball." He tips the cup to his lips. Frank continues, "My father wants me to be like him. A jock. He played football in college, and now my brother does."

"I don't know what my father wants," I reply.

"I don't want to be like him," Frank keeps on. "I don't want to play. I want to do what Whitey does."

He won't do anything after we get to Death Valley, if he's serious about the pact. But what if he changes his mind and doesn't do it? That'd be awful or good. I don't know which.

"So why don't you tell your dad that?" I ask.

Frank doesn't answer. He turns his head to the wall. I notice his ears turning red. I'm not sure if he's crying or mad.

I start to think about my father then. I wonder if my dad goes to baseball games and drinks beer. Then I wonder about whether he is a Giants fan in San Francisco. I don't want to think about him at all. Why is he in my head? I hate that!

This time I turn my face away from Frank. When he isn't looking, I bite my forearm. Hard. I can feel the teeth. Each one. No baseball. No dad. Just teeth. I clamp down and bite slow and harder each second, like a vise, more and more. It is so strong. Like taking a jump.

Then I feel the bruise starting under my skin.

And I don't think of anything.

April 20

Audrey: what is something really weird about yourself that no one knows?

Frank: i can't stand my father, but i respect him

Audrey: that is weird

Jin-Ae: owen?

Owen: i bite myself to make sure i'm not dead

Audrey: that is seriously messed up weird

Jin-Ae: i like how my farts smell

Frank: Noooooooooo!

Audrey: that's gross

Jin-Ae: u asked about weird

Audrey: but not disgusting

Audrey: i'm a compulsive liar

Jin-Ae: for real?

Audrey: no, i'm lying

THAT NIGHT WE RENT A HOTEL ROOM. FRANK SIGNS FOR IT WITH his dad's credit card and a fake ID. The room costs $249 for one night. We have two double beds and that makes me wonder who will sleep with whom.

As soon as we open the door to the room, Audrey shouts, "Shotgun shower." She throws her bag on the bed farthest from the door and heads straight to the bathroom.

"I gotta go!" yells Frank.

The bathroom door closes with a click. "Too late," says Audrey, her voice muffled through the door. "Use the lobby."

"Come on!" he yells much louder.

Audrey opens the door. "Only kidding."

I laugh. Frank gives her a dirty look, and then heads for the toilet. Jin-Ae drops her bag next to Audrey's, and that settles where we will all sleep.

"Think he'll spring for room service?" asks Jin-Ae.

Audrey looks at me. "Sounds like he had a good day, right?"

I smile. "Definitely."

Audrey grins. "Let's go for it. We can always pay cash."

Frank comes out of the bathroom while I'm holding the menu. Jin-Ae and Audrey, one on each side of me, seated on the bed, read along. "Starving," says Frank, and the issue is settled.

"I want a pizza—pepperoni and sausage," states Jin-Ae.

"Half," says Audrey. "Vegetarian, remember?"

"Okay."

"Let's have a party," says Frank. "I'm ordering some beer, too. Anyone else?"

"Can I get champagne?" Audrey asks. I'm surprised by that request.

Frank nods. Audrey glances over at Jin-Ae, who smiles broadly.

Suddenly I realize how hungry I feel. We've eaten poorly, bad schedule, too many Pop-Tarts. Hot dogs at Wrigley. "Chicken salad sandwich, French fries, Coke," I say.

"Call it in," says Frank with authority.

I haven't ever ordered room service. I feel nervous. Frank can tell. "Just dial and tell them what you want. The number is on the phone."

I end up ordering the pizza, my food, a big salad for Audrey, steaks for Jin-Ae and Frank, the fresh fruit plate, three beers, one Coke, a bottle of champagne, and a coffee for me.

I hang up. "Thirty minutes," I announce.

"Here," says Jin-Ae. Something flies at my face. I duck. Metal clinks against the wall.

"What—"

"Just put it on. Girl dogs got one for everybody."

"Us bitches," Audrey adds.

I turn and pick it up: a set of green dog tags on a long chain.

"We figured," Audrey says, "they were better than leashes and collars."

Etched onto the top tag are the words "Suicide Dogs."

"Besides," Audrey says with a grunt, "now they can identify our bodies easier."

I turn the metal and see "Professor Owen." I feel tears under my cheeks, sort of happy and sad together, but they don't surface.

Audrey goes into the bathroom for her shower.

"Did you convert Audrey to a lesbian at teen night?" Frank asks Jin-Ae, which sends my tears somewhere else. I slip the dog tags over my head. We start unpacking. I realize how dirty I feel. I want a shower, too.

Jin-Ae grins. "Not really. I think she was trying to convert some poor boy."

I pull off my sneakers. My feet smell. I'm a little embarrassed, but they've smelled worse in the car.

"What did you guys do before that?"

"We walked by the lake a long time. Ate at some place on the North Shore. I'm whupped."

I'm both tired and excited. The bed feels great.

"We made our lists," Jin-Ae says.

"Did you get to ten?" Frank asks.

"Nope. Only a few. But they're good ones. Champagne is on Audrey's list."

"Excellent!" Frank grins. He unzips his bag. I wonder if he's brought the gun inside or if it's still in the car. Frank turns on the television.

A few minutes later, I hear the bathroom door open. Audrey steps out wearing a towel around her middle, green dog tags around her neck. She looks shiny, still damp. The steam from the bathroom follows her into the room.

"We'll need more towels," Audrey says. "There's only one more in there." She walks toward her things. "Close your mouth, Owen," she says. I'm staring. I quickly turn away. Jin-Ae and Frank snicker.

Audrey gathers her things and dresses in the bathroom. I shower next. When I come out, the food is there. Frank already has ketchup on his chin.

I don't think I've ever had a better night.

We watch a Harry Potter movie, the first one, on television. We talk serious and mess around, jump on the beds, you name it.

Jin-Ae makes me write out a postcard for my mother from the Native American Educational Services College. I have no idea where she found it. "Just write," she says, "that you aren't going to go to this college."

"No kidding," I say.

Frank brings out a deck of cards. First we play twenty-one, but then after they all drink a little, Jin-Ae says we should play strip poker. I put my sneakers back on, because I don't know how to play. We don't play for too long. I lose the first five hands and take off my sneakers, socks, and belt. After that I don't lose again. No one ends up naked. Frank loses his sneakers and one sock. Jin-Ae loses the same. The last hand, Audrey loses. She says, "You're all chickens." She pulls off her shirt, right up over her head. She's wearing a purple bra. We can't play anymore after that, because we all hoot and holler, and I spill something on the cards. They throw stuff at me, like pizza and napkins.

Eventually each of them passes out one at a time. Jin-Ae, then Audrey, and then Frank falls asleep. I stay up watching TV. Every once in a while I think about Frank's gun. I go through his stuff while he's sleeping, looking for the pistol. But I don't find it.

Mostly, I keep thinking about Audrey in her bra, and that means I'm awake until four in the morning. While they're asleep, I remember the markers we bought and draw a little. The others don't stir.

Maybe we'll be like this at the end, together and sleeping after one good night.

April 21
Jin-Ae: ever feel really close to someone?
Frank: not really
Jin-Ae: that's what i want. what's missing in my life

Audrey: its worse to lose someone

Jin-Ae: i know. i told my best friend anna that i had a crush on her—on valentines day

Audrey: uh oh

Jin-Ae: it doesn't get worse than that kind of rejection

Audrey: amen sister

Frank: u 2 agree on something?

Audrey: yeah. we both think u r a jerk

THE ROOM IS A MESS, AS MY MOTHER WOULD SAY. EVEN WITH the curtains drawn and the lights out, I can tell. There's food on the floor, clothes everywhere. I hear the shower. I feel Frank next to me and see Audrey's shaved head nearby. Jin-Ae is the only one up, I guess. I grab a Coke and take a sip. That's left over from the second time we ordered room service—the dessert order.

I take the computer and Jin-Ae's phone, then head downstairs to the lobby. I accidentally dropped my phone in the toilet last week, before we left. For some reason I don't go on the Internet. Instead I call my mother. She picks up the phone after one ring.

"Hello?"

"Hi, Mom."

"Owen? I was getting worried about you." She always worries, even though I think I take better care of myself than she does.

"I'm fine."

"Owen. Is that really you? Oh boy, I've been missing you. How are you? Where are you?"

I find a couch and sit. Maybe I should have ordered coffee before I dialed. "Chicago."

"Chicago? Now?" Her voice is full of questions.

"Yes, I'm about to get some coffee."

"When did you start drinking coffee? Are you okay? When did you get to Chicago?"

"Mom, I'm fine. Trust me."

She doesn't really want me to answer all her questions. She just wants reassurance. "I'm not used to you being away. Or drinking coffee. What colleges are you looking at?"

"Didn't you get my e-mail, Mom? We were at Lehigh University two days ago."

"I haven't checked my e-mail lately."

"You should. It's easier for me to get a hold of you that way."

"Okay," she says softly.

For a moment we're silent. Her anxiety and questions pausing, maybe to regroup.

"I don't know where we're going today. Maybe the University of Chicago." That's also kind of true. Maybe. "We're going to Colorado next, I think."

"Did you like any of the colleges, Owen?"

I haven't thought about what to say to that question. "Lehigh was kind of fun. We saw the Eagles practice."

"Do you think, maybe, you'd like to go there?"

I don't know how to answer. She will have less to worry about soon. "I don't know, Mom." That's the truth.

"I wish you had your own phone, so I could find you easier. I don't like not being able to contact you."

"Just use this number then if you have to. But it's not my phone, so don't call unless it's an emergency, all right? Just e-mail."

"What else have you done, Owen? I miss you."

She always misses me. I wish she would go on a date or find a new hobby. It's time to move on with her life. I'm the only one really left at home, and no matter what, I will not be staying there.

"We went to a baseball game yesterday at Wrigley Field."

"You and Jin-Ae?"

"No, Frank."

"Frank?"

"Friend," I reply, feeling the power of the word.

"Wait until I tell Jimmy," she says.

"Yeah."

I picture her sitting at the kitchen table, coffee in front of her. That's where I do my homework, the center of our home, that's where I was—

"Your brother will pee himself," she says, her voice interrupting my thoughts, something that seemed important. "Was it fun?"

Surprisingly, when I think of it, I blurt, "Yes."

"Good for you. I'm glad you're having a good time. I didn't think I was ready for you to go away for so long, but I'm glad you're having fun. I better get used to it, since you're looking at colleges already."

Since you're gone. That's what she means even though she doesn't know it.

"I can't talk long, because it's not my phone."

In spite of myself, when she asks, I agree to call tomorrow or the next day.

"I love you, Owen," she says.

Although it takes me a second, I reply, "Me too."

I'm still not sure I know what love is, that I understand what it's like. I don't know if I love my father or not. Or my mother. I feel sad. I stay downstairs and drink coffee while I try to remember the kitchen table and everything my mother said, in case it's our last conversation.

April 22

Jin-Ae: my mother keeps saying i did it for attention

Owen: mr. clark said that to me too

Jin-Ae: he's a guidance counselor. what does he know?

Frank: maybe u did do it for attention

Jin-Ae: i don't want attention. i want to die

Audrey: then y aren't u dead?

Jin-Ae: they stopped me is y

*Frank: u make it sound so bad. everyone needs attention. i
wouldn't have tried if i got some attention from my dad*

Audrey: i never even met my dad

Frank: at least the right kind

*Owen: at Hastings they said a suicide attempt could be a
cry for help. that's what they said mine was.*

*Jin-Ae: my mother makes it sound like all i'm doing is trying
to get attention*

Audrey: r u?

*Jin-Ae: NO! i hate the way she's all embarrassed by me.
don't shame our family. i hate the way they tell me who
to be and how i'm not what they want. i hate myself. i
don't know why*

Audrey: maybe u should hate them instead

THE DOOR TO THE ROOM IS LOCKED. I HAVE TO KNOCK BECAUSE
I forgot the key.

Audrey opens the door. "Nice face." She grins. I forgot
about the markers. She's half-dressed, a T-shirt and pajama
bottoms. I play dumb. Everyone is awake.

The room seems more organized. Jin-Ae appears the most

ready to go. Plates in hand, she piles dishes near the television. Her zipped bag rests on the bed.

I look at Frank, the blue stripes running vertically down his face. "What's with the lines?" I ask.

"Aha," says Jin-Ae, pointing at Audrey. "I knew it was you."

"No, really," Audrey protests.

"I had a rainbow and gay pride written on my forehead," Jin-Ae says.

I have to pretend again. Quickly, I run over to the mirror. Black lines stretch sideways across my face from ear to ear. I fake disgust.

"Audrey is the culprit," Jin-Ae says. "The only one without any marks."

Audrey shakes her head in denial. I make a pretend mean face at her. The best way to avoid getting caught is to make yourself one of the victims.

Frank looks hungover again. Drinking doesn't seem to do him well. The stripes make him look sicker. He moves slowly across the room. "I'm taking a shower," he grumbles.

"No coffee or Danish for us?" Audrey asks.

I hadn't thought of it. She opens the door again. "Go get us some coffee, zebra head."

Her voice isn't angry, it's silly, even though I know she's serious.

"None for me," says Jin-Ae.

"Bring some for Frank," Audrey continues, gently pushing

me out the door. "He needs it, even if he says he doesn't. Make it black. Just get out of here so I can finish getting changed."

"Anything else?" I ask as she closes the door behind me. I think that I'm getting a crush on her.

April 24
Owen: i would like to meet u all
Frank: same
Audrey: luv 2. work something out

THE ROAD IS SO LONG. JUST STRAIGHT THROUGH IOWA AND Nebraska, long and straight and empty in the middle. We have to drive about 1,192 miles from Chicago to Woody Creek, Colorado. Not much to see but flat. Just us in the car. That's enough, I think. But even that can get boring.

WHAT IS NOT BORING IN THE CAR IS AUDREY. SOMETHING IS different now. Like when she puts her legs across my lap, I feel nervous, but a strange nervous, kind of happy. Before it was nervous because I didn't know her. Now I want to know her more, and I'm afraid I won't. That kind of nervous.

Near Des Moines, Frank says, "Can we play movies on that computer?"

"Sure," I reply.

"Let's get some."

We drive off Interstate 80 and into the city, which is not really a city at all. Only suburbia, in a way. At least the part I see. Maybe the big part is farther off. Maybe we are in the suburbs.

When we stop, I'm the last one out of the car again. "I need to put on my shoes," I tell them. They walk away toward the store. I slowly reach under the seat. I feel the gun still there.

I cry a little then, gasping. I wish I didn't cry so much. I don't know what to do. I feel things that I haven't felt before, and I don't know why.

I am remembering my father. I am hanging on his leg, begging.

"Daddy," I cry. We stand in the living room, in the dark. He's yelling at my mother, or maybe me.

Suddenly I'm banging my head on the parking lot outside of Frank's car. I can feel the hurt. There's something good about it. Mostly it makes me stop remembering.

JIN-AE SPOTS ME IN THE STORE. FRANK AND AUDREY AREN'T in sight.

"What happened to you?" she says.

I know she means my forehead. I can feel the bruising.

"I hit my head on the ground," I reply softly. I want to tell her about the gun.

But before I can say another word, she blurts, "Klutz."

I don't correct her. Instead I shrug. I'll tell her later.

Frank arrives with all three Lord of the Rings movies, which makes me feel much better. Audrey shows up with *28 Days Later*, a horror flick that I like. They both look at my head.

"Goofy fell out of the car and cracked his head." Jin-Ae laughs. Frank doesn't react. Audrey scrunches up her face, but doesn't say anything.

Next, we go to Starbucks and each e-mail home again. No one wants to talk to his or her family on the phone.

Audrey leans over to me while Frank is typing. She's drinking an iced coffee. "Here," she says, putting the cup against my bruised head. The cold sends shivers all over. I don't remember anyone ever doing that for me, not even my mom. Then Jin-Ae brings me ice for my forehead. They're so nice.

When it's my turn to e-mail, I Google Frank's father instead. He has a business called Falzone's Imports, Web site and everything. They seem successful. I wonder if they sell guns.

Shopping and e-mail done, we're back on the road within an hour, watching *The Fellowship of the Ring*.

Top Ten Biggest Not-Suicide Deaths We Can Think Of

    10. *Challenger* disaster

     9. *Hindenburg* explosion

     8. Wreck of the *Titanic*

7. Great fire of Chicago

6. San Francisco earthquake

5. Katrina floods in New Orleans

4. Tsunami in Asia

3. Hiroshima/Nagasaki atomic bombs

2. Holocaust

1. Meteor that killed the dinosaurs

April 27

Jin-Ae: they're holding another school assembly
about suicide this week. and one for parents on
thursday night

Owen: how come?

Jin-Ae: probably b/c they don't want anyone to kill themselves b/c of us owen

Owen: do we get to go?

Jin-Ae: i'm going to be sick from school that day

Owen: i want to go

Jin-Ae: WHY?!

Owen: i think it's interesting. do u all want to come?
we could finally meet in person

Jin-Ae: u sound desperate, like a sexual predator owen

Owen: that's not funny

Frank: it's three hours drive from westchester owen.
think of something else

Audrey: can't. sorry

Jin-Ae: oh well

Owen: maybe we could all go to the movies together some weekend

Audrey's foot wakes me up. She nudges me in the chest.

"Owen, come on."

I'm surprised that I've fallen asleep.

"We need you for this part."

I'm groggy. "What?"

"Time for secrets."

I yawn and stretch. She kicks me, lightly, in the chest again. "Owen!"

"I'm awake."

The sun is down. I can't see much but the lights of cars on the highway. The laptop rests on the back window. Frank drives. Jin-Ae twists halfway around in the front seat, leaning against the door, to look back at Audrey and me.

"We want to hear your wish list, Owen. We wrote ours in Chicago. So now it's your turn," says Jin-Ae. "Group sharing."

"Can't I smoke a cigarette, Frank?" asks Audrey.

"Fine! I'm tired of you bugging me. Just keep the window down."

"Yes!" She fumbles in her bag.

"We want to know, Owen!" continues Jin-Ae.

Audrey takes out a pack of cigarettes, rolls the window down, and lights one.

"I didn't do a list."

"So do one now. Pretend we're in group therapy."

Frank interrupts. "Give him a break."

"Oh, come on," Audrey says. "It's no big deal."

"That's because you didn't get yours read out loud. Yours wasn't a secret."

"You haven't heard it yet, so it's still a secret."

"But," he says, "you knew when you wrote it that you were going to tell. So that's like cheating. Not really secret."

"You're pissed about the sex one on yours." Jin-Ae laughs.

I can feel Frank's embarrassment from the backseat, but I smile anyway. "I didn't do it," I repeat. Audrey nudges me with her elbow, blows smoke out the window at the same time.

"You can make something up, Professor," Jin-Ae insists.

"Why don't you start?" Frank challenges her.

"Fine."

One of the things that therapists do if you are suicidal, like a trick, is ask you about the future. They want to know what your plans are. Do you want to be the president? Do you want to be a rock star? They want to know if you want to live later even if you want to die now. Mr. Clark, the school counselor, told that to me a few times. He said, "I'm worried about you because you don't seem to have any plans for the future, no goals. Isn't there anything you want?" I usually answer him, "Not really."

Audrey takes a long, slow drag on her cigarette. The red end glows as she inhales.

"Why do you smoke if you're a vegetarian?" Frank asks before Jin-Ae starts.

"These are vegetarian cigarettes."

He shakes his head. "Seriously."

"Addicted, I guess," Audrey mumbles. "I'm trying to stop."

April 27

Audrey: u study suicide?

Owen: yes

Audrey: u sound addicted to it

Owen: idk

Audrey: maybe we should name ourselves suicide anonymous

"ALL RIGHT, WHAT THE HECK," SAYS JIN-AE DRAMATICALLY. "I want to have sex. That's the first thing on my list!"

"You already said that," Frank mutters.

"No," she says. "I mean, like, fall in love, have sex. I want to meet someone who is gay—"

"We did that at gay bingo," Audrey interrupts.

"Shhh. It's my list. So listen."

No one speaks. Audrey takes another drag on her cigarette.

"I want to meet someone and fall in love. Not Savannah, not Anna. Someone who will love me back. I want to be in a relationship. Go to the gay prom in New York or Philly."

"That ain't happening before Death Valley," mumbles Frank.

"Up yours," she says. "I want someone who is gay for a relationship. Go to dinner or on a date. And I want to . . ." Her voice trails off, then booms, "I wish I was straight sometimes. It would be so much easier. Give me a cigarette."

Audrey leans forward. "You don't smoke."

"Well, I'm starting now. This secrets crap was a bad idea."

We all laugh. Audrey takes her cigarette and holds it to Jin-Ae's mouth. Jin-Ae inhales, and then coughs explosively. We laugh harder. Jin-Ae gags. I expect her to vomit.

"*That*," Audrey hoots, "was a bad idea."

Even Jin-Ae chuckles.

"What else is on your list?" asks Frank, after a moment. "Break it out. Let Owen read it out loud."

"No need. It's short. I want to visit Korea. See where I came from."

"Can't do that on this trip," Frank answers back.

"Then maybe I'll have to kill myself some other suicide trip," she counters.

I'm confused about our pack and our pact now. All the things Jin-Ae wants are so far away. Maybe she's not serious.

Outside, I see the small stalks of corn in the dark. It will not be ready for harvest for a long time, time we'll never see. I wonder if we tried to end the trip, turn back, call off the whole thing, if Frank would shoot us with his gun, and leave us out here in Nebraskansas.

Mr. Clark made me sign something once about how if I wanted to hurt myself, I'd call him first. Gave me his home number. I never called. The number went in the toilet with my cell phone. He'll be pretty disappointed later.

Audrey tosses her cigarette butt out the window. Through the back windshield I see sparks like tiny fireworks as it hits the pavement behind us. "Gee, this is fun," she says.

I don't like how they're fighting. I ask, "What else is on your list?"

Audrey answers before Jin-Ae can. "You already heard. She wants to be a doctor or lawyer. Something important. Successful. Make her family proud through hard work. But you can't do that when you're dead."

I don't answer. Audrey rolls up her window. Frank doesn't speak either.

"That's true," says Jin-Ae. "So who cares? Your turn, Audrey."

"No problem," she responds. "Stop smoking."

"Ha!" yells Frank.

"Drink champagne. But I did that already. Thank you, Frank, for that!"

I notice that his shoulders drop, relaxing, but he doesn't say anything.

"I also want to learn how to play the guitar, even though I don't have one. I want to drive too. Go to a concert. Get a tattoo. And I want to change the world. Like, have people treat each other right. Stop the oil companies from starting wars in Iraq. And end hunger."

"Nothing too big there," Jin-Ae quips.

Audrey leans back, throws her feet up onto me. That gesture makes me catch my breath.

"The hardest one I just added."

"What's that?" Jin-Ae asks.

"I think I would like to try to forgive my father and visit him in jail."

"You are very intense, girlfriend," Jin-Ae replies.

"Any chance you want to drive me to Florida, Frank?" Audrey asks.

He laughs. I know it's my turn next. They wait for me to speak.

April 28

Jin-Ae: watz it like when yur dead?

Owen: quiet. no noise. no words

"I don't have anything," I say after a long moment.

Audrey rubs her feet on my chest again, playfully. "Come on, Your Majesty. Nothing?"

Frank turns his head, looking back at me. "Think of something, Owen."

I reach out my hands and stroke Audrey's feet. She makes a noise, sort of purring. Like a shock, I find myself talking. "I want a kiss," I say. "I have never kissed anyone."

Audrey leans forward, kisses my cheek.

Frank laughs quietly.

"No," I say, breathless, gently pushing her back. "I mean, a real kiss. Like, from someone who likes me."

Audrey starts to lean forward again. I find myself stopping her with my hand.

"For real," I say firmly. I don't let them see my hands shaking.

"That's sweet, Owen," says Jin-Ae.

Audrey reaches out, takes my arm. "Tell you what, Owen. You think of a few more things you want to do"—she pauses. I can feel my heart pounding—"and I'll be your girlfriend for the trip."

I don't know how to respond to that one.

"Oh yeah," squeals Jin-Ae.

Frank howls. "Oo, ooooo." His head tilts back.

Jin-Ae joins in with a howl of her own. Then Audrey enters the racket. "Ooo, oooo," she barks in my ear.

I lean away. I feel the car accelerating along with Frank's adrenaline. We are definitely speeding. I reach out, impulsively, and stroke Audrey's hair, her fuzz, her scar.

"Ooooo-wen," she howls.

My mouth doesn't open, but wants to.

"Ooooo-wen."

Then Jin-Ae turns to look at me. Audrey pokes me. From the front Frank's voice changes. "Oooooooo-wen."

And my heart feels scratching, clawing, a physical sensation from the ribs out, a pawing in the dirt of me.

In unison the three of them shout my name in a long, howling call. A summons.

I am surprised by the answer. My own head tilts back, releasing a sound I've never known, something ancient. No cages. No moon. My throat feels alive. It's just the highway and the sound of suicide rushing out the windows.

Then Frank turns off the headlights.

Simply darkness.

THIS, I THINK, IS HOW WE DIE. FRANK KILLS US ALL.

In the distance, the lights of another car come into view, outlining Frank and Jin-Ae in the front seat, the open road in front of us. The howling ends.

And Frank turns the headlights back on.

Audrey applauds.

April 29

Audrey: 2 bad u guys couldnt come to nyc

Frank: y?

Owen: you mean so we could be together?

Audrey: class trip to the opera. walked around the city

Jin-Ae: u like opera?

Audrey: madam butterfly. suicide opera. standing ovation

Jin-Ae: thought u were in a wheelchair

Audrey: it wasn't as bad as they thought

Jin-Ae: oh

WE TRAVEL FOR ABOUT ANOTHER HOUR. FRANK ASKS US TO PLAY the radio. I think he's too tired to drive much more. Eventually we see an exit with a campground sign a few miles down the road. The campground is only a field with some picnic tables, grills, and a bathroom building. Once again, Audrey and I will share the tent. Frank and Jin-Ae go off in search of where to register.

I grab the pillows and our blankets. Mosquitoes swarm around my forehead and my bruise, biting tonight, so I want to get in the tent as soon as possible. Audrey unwraps the bag and tosses it toward me. A quick pull, and the tent springs open.

"I wish we had air mattresses," she says, throwing pillows inside. She pauses for a moment to rub her head, fingers tapping along the scar.

"Me too," I reply.

"Head hurt?"

"A little."

"You should take some aspirin."

We watch the light from Frank's flashlight grow bigger as they return. "No store. Just showers," says Jin-Ae.

"We're going out for breakfast tomorrow," adds Frank. "If we can find a town."

Audrey and I climb into the tent. I hear the car doors close. I wonder if the bugs will make sleeping in the car with the windows open difficult. We share one small flashlight for settling our things. I sleep in my T-shirt and shorts. Audrey goes through some contortions and pulls her bra off, not the purple one, without removing her shirt. She's also in shorts and a T-shirt.

"Maybe if we put both sleeping bags on the ground it won't be so bad," she whispers. The floor feels bumpy, but not too hard. Hard earth, not stones. "Besides, it's not cold tonight. We can share one blanket on top."

"Okay." I haven't ever shared a blanket with a girl, except in the car. Last time we each rolled up in our own blankets. We move the covers and pillows. Then she turns off the light.

For a long time I don't move. I don't think I breathe at all. I'm petrified of being so close to her and of brushing up against her. Instead, I count her breaths, up to one hundred. Then I start over again. She lies on her side, facing me. After a while my sight adjusts and I can see her closed eyes. Her breathing is regular, once about every five seconds.

"Audrey," I whisper, real soft.

Being so close to her face makes me want to talk to her, to tell her. I don't let faces get that close, at least not often. She breathes shallow and slow. I'm thinking back to something she asked a long time ago before we started this trip, back in our IMs. She doesn't, but she does, know about me. I want to keep her.

April 30

Audrey: u didn't answer my question. y do u keep trying to kill yourself?

Owen: i can't tell u

Audrey: y not?

Owen: i just cant

Audrey: i told u everyone has a secret

Her breathing is completely even and regular. I try not to move.

"Do you really think everyone has a secret?" I say aloud.

She doesn't answer. I don't expect her to. I don't really want her to wake up. But maybe telling her my secret will bind her to me, even in her dreams.

"Listen," I say again, softer. "I'll tell you my secret, okay?"

Again, nothing, only steady slow breathing.

"I never told anyone—"

I pretend she's awake. Her face is close to me. Like Forrest. Like when I was little.

"My brother Forrest was seven years older than me, fourteen when he died. James, my other brother, was eleven." I pause, waiting, but she doesn't move.

"James had a baseball tournament, and my parents went to see his game. Forrest and me were playing in the backyard, in the pool. I was swimming and knew how to swim pretty well, even though I was only supposed to stay in the shallow end of the pool when my parents weren't home. I remember it was very hot, and school was out, and we were going to go somewhere for the Fourth of July weekend after my parents and James got home. They said that we could go camping."

I stop, quiet, listening for noises outside. I realize I am talking so fast that I have a hard time breathing. Nervous.

"Forrest and I were home alone and swimming in the pool. Jumping around. Doing cannonballs. He climbed out of the pool to go get a soda from the porch. That's when I swam out in the deep end. I started splashing around, my arms real loud, making waves. Then I pretended, yelling, 'Forrest, help me. I'm drowning. Forrest, I can't swim.'

"He came running, real fast, across the porch, and then I

crash into me ✳ 129

thought he was going to dive in. Only he sort of stepped and fell in, feet first, like a slide, with his butt crashing real big, a giant splash. I figured he knew I was joking and that he was trying to cannonball me. Only then I thought maybe he didn't know I was joking. Then I knew he was joking, because he just lay there with his face in the water, pretending to drown."

Slowly I roll onto my back, careful not to touch Audrey. I lower my voice. I don't want Frank or Jin-Ae to hear me. Now, the words come real slow.

"I kept on splashing my arms, saying, 'Forrest, help me.' But he kept his face in the water. I got tired and said, 'You win,' and I swam over to him and grabbed him, only he didn't move. That's when I saw the big cut on his head, on the back of his head, and the blood starting to float around his face in the water. No one else was there, but I kept on yelling, 'Forrest, Forrest!' I think he fell and hit his head when he was jumping in after me. I remember yelling at him, and telling him to stop playing, and trying to wake him up. But he didn't move. Then I tried to pull his face out of the water, only he was so heavy. And I tried to pull him over to the ladder, but he was so heavy, and I was getting so tired. I kept picking up his face, trying to get him to breathe, yelling at him and looking in his eyes. They were open and red with the chemicals from the water. I told him I would bite him if he didn't knock it off, and then I did bite him right on the ear to try and wake him.

I kept getting tired and hanging on him like a raft and trying to pull him to the wall, and once or twice I went over to the edge and tried to lift him out, but I couldn't lift him. Finally, I climbed out. I laid on the edge of the pool and kept his head in my hands, trying to hold him up with his face out of the water. I held him there, leaning over the edge with my body on the concrete, yelling, 'Forrest, wake up!' I kept on biting him too. I didn't know what else to do. And so much time went by, so long. Then somehow I raised his chin up onto the edge, and I knew he was dead. He wasn't breathing. It was awful. He was dead."

Audrey's breathing hasn't changed. I inhale deep and slow, then keep talking.

"So I left him there. And I ran inside, because I didn't want to get in trouble. I changed my clothes and went and pretended I didn't know what had happened and sat in front of the TV until my parents came home and found him.

"Later, I heard my mom say how if they had been here, they could probably have saved him. Called the ambulance. Given him CPR. But my dad said his neck was broken.

"No one knows I was there and couldn't save him. I did it. I did it by pretending to drown, so that he jumped bad and hit his head, thinking I was in trouble. And then I couldn't save him."

"Is that why you bite your arm?" Audrey says, shocking me with her voice.

I can't see her face. I've been looking straight up into the dark. "You're awake?"

"Is that why you bite yourself? Because you bit him and he didn't wake up?"

"I—I—I never thought of that," I say, trembling at her voice. I'm very rapidly aware of shame.

"Besides," she says firmly, "you didn't do it. You tried to save him, but you were just a kid. He jumped, not you."

"I did it, really."

"Trust me, Owen. That's not true. He made a mistake. That doesn't mean you *both* should be dead."

"Maybe we are. And this is a bad dream, like hell."

"You're not dead." Audrey laughs.

"How do you know?" I practically shout, feeling a wave of guilt and anger, something hot.

Suddenly I feel her hands on me. She bites my forearm.

I wince.

"Sorry," she whispers. All of a sudden, I find myself holding her. She reaches her hands behind me. I place my hand on the back of her head and feel the short hair of her buzz cut. Her smell grabs me. Inside of me something happens. I lean forward to kiss her. All at once, her tongue is in my mouth. I feel, as best I can describe it, hungry.

We kiss.

"Told you that you weren't dead," she whispers.

I kiss her again while she tries to speak.

"Gentle," she says, like a command. She bites me, a nibble on the lips. Then we're too busy to speak for a long, long time.

May 2

Audrey: if you love something that's the only way to survive

Jin-Ae: love and grief are inseparable according to the poets

SHE'S STILL SLEEPING. I CANNOT BELIEVE I'M HERE WITH HER now. I probably sound stupid and corny, I think I'm in love. That was the best night of my life. I didn't know anything could be like that. The best part is that I cried a lot, but she didn't care. And I cried because I was happy, and because of Forrest, and because of Audrey and I don't know why. Audrey is a very good kisser, and that is not all. Wow.

I think the best time I ever had before this was maybe Christmas when I was little, about four or five years old. Santa Claus still brought things, and that year I asked for a bicycle. A real one, like my brothers both had, not the three-wheel kind. And I remember on Christmas morning I found my bike right next to the tree. I jumped around, and then I climbed up on the couch, and I dove off right into my father's arms. We still lived in California with no snow. I made them all come outside with me to watch me ride. I don't think I did so well, but I didn't care either. I remember yelling, "Jimmy, look at me." Forrest tried to help me too, running next to me. They didn't put training wheels on that bike because they thought I could do it on my own. And I did.

That's sort of what it felt like to be with Audrey last night. I know that sounds stupid, but I don't care, either.

Like Christmas, I want everyone to know. But I also want to keep this one for myself. Not share it with anyone.

I'm in a very good mood.

May 8

Frank: what's the best thing that ever happened to u?

Jin-Ae: say yours first

Frank: ok—when we went to the NBA finals

Audrey: a basketball game?????

Frank: the finals! my dad took me and my brother and my
cousin

Jin-Ae: when

Frank: when the nets were playing. they won at home. it was
great. wat about u guys?

Audrey: there's so many

Audrey: when my stepfather finally went to jail

Audrey: when we moved for the third time in seventh grade

Audrey: after i broke both legs jumping off the roof

Audrey: the time my boyfriend screwed me over and
dumped me for some girl he just met. now that was
definitely the best thing that ever happened to me

Frank: sorry i asked

Audrey: no, i mean it. i'm glad for all of them. made me a
stronger person

Jin-Ae: i won the poetry slam on shakespeare's birthday

Owen: what is that?

Jin-Ae: poetry contest. only you read poems out loud. like
american idol

Jin-Ae: y are u always last owen?

Owen: what do u mean?

Jin-Ae: last to say something

Owen: don't have anything to say

Jin-Ae: so what? make something up. what's your best thing?

Owen: idk. don't think i have one

Audrey: pick something

Owen: i liked it the first time i went to hastings hospital. they
were nice there

Jin-Ae: u have got to be kidding!

Owen: NO. i got it. when the third Lord of the Rings movie
came out. i went to see all three movies in a row. that
was great

Audrey: geek. just kidding. lov u

I wake up in the backseat to Audrey drawing a snake on my arm with permanent marker.

"You know what they say about paybacks." She laughs as Frank and Jin-Ae glance back from the front seat. I let her finish without a word. "I came up with a special plan, for Jin-Ae," she continues, snapping the cap onto the marker. The snake on my arm winds from my elbow to my wrist, striped.

"Oh goody." Jin-Ae smirks.

"Seriously, I read a book on Wiccan and Druidic stuff."

"Druidic *stuff*?" Jin-Ae says.

I turn my wrist, and the snake seems to move, come alive, dancing. Neat.

"Shh. Listen for a change," says Audrey. Jin-Ae rolls her eyes, but doesn't speak. "Snakes are symbols of change. 'Transmutation' is the word. We're going to transmute you on this trip, Jin-Ae."

Jin-Ae sighs loudly.

"Which means what?" asks Frank.

"Help you get over your fear of being gay."

"I'm not afraid," Jin-Ae says.

"You're scared of your family's reaction."

Audrey uncaps the marker again. She signals to me with her head, silently, asking for my other arm. I hold it out toward her.

"So?" says Jin-Ae.

"So it's time for you to stop being afraid of your mommy."

This time the marker tickles a little as she places the tip on the inside part of my bicep. She's holding two markers, red and black, writing on me with the black. I watch the dragon slowly take shape: large head, black with red eyes, tongue, and fire. The body wraps around my bicep and down onto my forearm, tail all the way across the back of my hand. The dragon dances when I move my arm. She draws better than me, better than I would have guessed.

"Won't matter," Jin-Ae says, "by the time we get to the desert."

"Matters now."

"Markers stink," says Frank. All the windows are already down.

"Shirt," Audrey says to me, lifting her chin.

I don't move. She raises her chin again. I lift off my shirt, stuff it next to me on the seat.

"You got it bad, Owen." Jin-Ae laughs.

Audrey uncaps the red marker. She turns to Jin-Ae. "Everybody gets tattooed today. None of that blame-Audrey-in-the-hotel stuff. I didn't draw on your faces."

"I never—"

"Don't bother," Frank interrupts Jin-Ae, touching her arm. "She's on a roll today. It'll wash off."

"Eventually. 'Permanent' means 'really hard to scrub off your skin.' "

Audrey leans over, close to me again. Her hand rests against my bare chest. I feel myself, skinny and puny. My heart races. In spite of the warm weather, I feel myself tremble, chill. She draws a small heart about the size of a quarter over my heart, writes "Audrey" in black letters. I grin. She tugs playfully on my dog tags.

"One more," she whispers softly.

Again I nod without speaking, remembering her touch from last night. With the black marker, she begins to make large, bold letters across my torso.

"You're not putting any battleship or dragon on my chest." Jin-Ae grunts. Frank and I chuckle.

"Don't laugh," Audrey says to me, pushing my chest to stop my movement. "You'll mess this up."

I exhale loudly.

"Dragons," Audrey tells us, "at least from Druidic legends, are the same as snakes. Wise. Old. About initiation."

"*Beowulf,*" says Frank. "Studied it in English this year."

"*The Hobbit,*" I say. "Bilbo defeated the dragon." Audrey moves the marker lower, for another word.

"Yeah, yeah, yeah" says Jin-Ae. "I don't want a hobbit or Beowulf tattoo. I don't—"

"Snake it is then," Audrey interrupts. Jin-Ae doesn't object this time. When Audrey finishes writing on my chest, I pull my shirt back on. The dragon and snake on my arms stick out of my short sleeves. I like how they look.

Awkwardly, without Frank stopping the car, Jin-Ae and I switch seats. Her turn to be marked. She climbs in back first. I scramble up front. I realize then that we're not on the interstate anymore. The road is just two lanes, relatively empty.

Audrey points to the billboard up ahead. Snakeland. Five miles.

I turn to look at Jin-Ae's growing tattoo. A small snake, on her ankle. All red.

May 13

Jin-Ae: i became suicidal in biology class, tenth grade

Audrey: ?

Jin-Ae: my teacher told us that snakes can get trapped in their own skin. they grow but don't have what it takes to burst through the old skin. they get sick inside and die

Frank: that made u suicidal?

Jin-Ae: the only way that kind of snake can survive is to crash itself against the rocks, like not care if it lives anymore. then it can live. but it has to flail around so bad, smash itself up

Audrey: u can't come out can u?

Jin-Ae: that's like a trick question right?

Top Ten Places to Visit That Aren't Graves

10. Liverpool, England, birthplace of the Beatles

    (Audrey's idea)

9. Key West, Florida, gay town (my idea for Jin-Ae)

8. Death Valley, California (!)

7. Coliseum, Rome, Italy (Frank's idea)

6. Britt, Iowa, National Hobo Convention (Audrey's idea)

5. Stonehenge, England, pagan site for Audrey (Frank's idea)

4. Area 51, Roswell, New Mexico (My idea)

3. Titan Missile Museum, Green Valley, Arizona (Frank's idea)

2. Wigstock, New York City, transvestite festival

    (Audrey's idea)

1. Icelandic Phallological (Penis) Museum, Iceland

    (Jin-Ae's idea)

FOR AN OUT-OF-THE-WAY PLACE, SNAKELAND LOOKS FAIRLY crowded. Maybe it's the only tourist spot around. The gift shop includes posters of snakes, snakeskin clothing, temporary tattoos, rubber snakes, even canned snake. I don't want anything. The main attraction, the snake exhibit, houses more than one hundred different varieties. Frank buys us all tickets from a woman wearing a blue rattlesnake T-shirt.

"Ever been bit?" asks Frank.

"Quite a bit," she replies, then giggles at her own pun.

"She's a dyke," Audrey chimes in, pointing at Jin-Ae who is obviously startled.

The woman hands Frank our tickets, looks at all of us. Audrey continues, "Can't tell her parents."

"Why should she?" asks the lady.

"Why'd you do that?" Jin-Ae says angrily. She stomps off toward the snakes. Audrey shrugs.

I walk into the exhibit with Frank, whose tattoo is also a snake, also on his forearm. His isn't as skinny as mine, though. Big and full, it's wrapped around a rose that runs straight from his wrist to his elbow. Audrey walks fast, seeking Jin-Ae.

The snakes in cages lie very still. Most look asleep. I don't know if they sleep or not. From what I understand, snakes prefer hot desert, not Colorado. Then, as if in answer to my question, there's a sign explaining all the details of hibernation during the cold months and how Snakeland keeps the heat up all year round.

I imagined the place would be a dump—dirty, dusty, something old and left over from the 1960s, with faded paint. Instead the exhibit room is amazing. Full-size murals line the walls. A giant, stone cobra head, much like the one at the Philadelphia Zoo, marks the entrance.

We catch up with the girls. Audrey is saying, "Other people have crap too. They live through it. You're not the only one who has ever had trouble coming out to their folks."

"It's not just that," Jin-Ae says softly, sitting down on one of the benches. Frank slows. I can tell he's trying to decide if we should stop or not.

I look at the wall. Adam and Eve stare down from a big picture behind the girls. A small sign explains, "Christian tradition suggests that the Devil took the form of a snake who tempted the first humans. Without the serpent symbol of evil, humans would never have left paradise."

Frank leans forward as if to say something. I kick his foot, gently, stopping him. He nods.

Audrey presses, "So what if they don't like who you are. Say, 'Mom, Dad. I'm gay.'"

"They'll disown me."

"You're dead in a thousand miles anyway."

"I can't deal with the rejection."

"Maybe if you tell them, you stop rejecting yourself. You want to die a liar?"

Frank and I keep walking. In one of the cages farther up, about forty crickets jump around in the container with two copperheads.

"Audrey won't like that," Frank comments under his breath.

The snakes don't move, but the crickets bounce like crazy. They know they are doomed.

OUTSIDE, JUST BEFORE WE OPEN THE CAR DOORS TO LEAVE, Frank turns to me. "I never saw your big tattoo, Owen."

I lift my shirt. Suddenly, I don't feel puny. I puff out my chest. In black letters, big enough for me to read in the reflection of the car window, shines Audrey's quote: "Suicide is confession."

May 15

Frank: how come only me n jin-ae put our pictures on
    the web?
Audrey: no camera
Owen: shy, i guess

WE SHOULD BE IN WOODY CREEK, COLORADO, IN LESS than one hour. Hunter S. Thompson, the writer, shot himself in the head there on February 20, 2005. He lived in a fortified compound. They fired his ashes out of a giant cannon in Aspen. I haven't been able to find out the exact address of his compound in Woody Creek. I also don't have any ritual for us to do when we get there.

I don't have any real interest in going to where he died anymore. I don't think I ever did. We're stopping here because it's on the way to Hemingway's grave, and then to Seattle. And I had to pick someone. There is no grave I want to visit.

I don't think I'm suicidal anymore. I thought I was definitely going to do it even if the others didn't. Maybe you can't be suicidal if you're in love. I will probably have to do it anyway. We made a deal.

Jin-Ae starts talking, as if she can read my mind. "Who all still wants to kill themselves?" she asks out loud. She raises her hand halfway. "I do, kind of."

Frank says, "Sort of."

"Seriously," Jin-Ae continues, "if I have to go home, I will definitely off myself. I cannot imagine going back there."

"That's different than wanting to kill yourself," Audrey says.

"True, but . . ." She inhales deeply. "I can't remember feeling this free. Like I'm somebody else."

"Maybe you are. Can I smoke again, Frank?"

"Thought you were quitting."

"I'm trying."

"Window open," he says. Audrey obliges.

The scenery has changed dramatically from Iowa and Nebraska. We're in the woods now, traveling along Highway 82, toward the valley. Woody Creek is only eight miles from Aspen, Colorado's big tourist area. Woody Creek isn't like that, though. It's not even a town.

"You don't have to stay there," Audrey says to Jin-Ae. "You could move here. Or Chicago. Don't you go to college next year?"

"Next year," Jin-Ae says with a grunt.

"Just a year," says Audrey.

"I can't take that."

"You took it so far."

Jin-Ae doesn't have an answer.

"Are you suicidal still?" Frank asks Audrey.

"What do you think?" Audrey replies, not answering.

I smile and put my hand on Audrey's ankle. The movement comes naturally.

"Maybe I am," she says, slowly.

Audrey and I make eye contact.

"Or maybe not."

"Good for you," Frank says, gruffly.

"Nobody stays suicidal forever." Audrey's voice is calm. "You either die or you get over it."

May 16

Frank: i think u r right about us needing to meet in person owen

Owen: y

Frank: bc then maybe audrey wouldnt have tried to kill herself by jumping off the roof

Jin-Ae: think so?

Audrey: no

WOODY CREEK IS BOTH WOODS AND WATER—TREES AND A river. There are a few roads, a trailer park, a couple stores, the Woody Creek Tavern.

"How will we find where he lives?" asks Frank.

"Lived," corrects Jin-Ae. "Just drive around."

"Can't we walk around?" asks Audrey. "I'm sick of sitting in a car."

"Actually, that's a good idea." Frank parks at the end of the full parking lot for the tavern. For an out of the way place, lots of cars and trucks are here.

The town seems weird. I see gun racks in the back of a few trucks, but also antiwar bumper stickers. The sun throws late afternoon shadows. I figure it's five o'clock.

"Are we going to eat anything?" I ask.

"Definitely," Frank replies.

Once again, I'm last out of the car. I slide my hand under the seat and feel the gun.

"Freak show," Frank comments as we approach the building. I know what he means. A big dolphin is nailed to the outside wall. I spy a small white figure next to a black pig on the roof. I can't tell if it's a dancing leprechaun or one of the animals from *The Lion King*. In the back, a giant rocking horse, part of a carousel, stands on the deck.

Aside from the stools at the bar, the tavern looks more like a restaurant. We claim the last empty table.

"Cute," says Jin-Ae, pointing to a can of SPAM nailed to the wall.

"I bet everybody knew this guy. He was famous," Audrey whispers. "What's his name?"

I nod. "Wrote for *Rolling Stone* magazine."

"Screwed up guy, right?" asks Frank. "Lots of drugs?"

"Yes."

Our waitress comes over with four menus. She is lean, with long brown hair tied back. No apron, only a pair of jeans and tie-dyed shirt. She tells us her name is Heather and rattles off some special about trout with almonds. When Frank orders a beer, she checks his ID.

"Fake, you know," she says, holding the card and looking Frank right in the eye.

He tilts his head like a question. Of course, he doesn't say anything. I never thought he could pass for twenty-one.

"You can tell. Not by the card." She smiles. "It's them." She lifts her chin, pointing to Audrey and me. "They're way too young to be out with you." She hands back the card.

"Sweet," says Jin-Ae after she leaves.

Frank shrugs. "She could've kept it."

Audrey finds vegetarian nachos. Frank and Jin-Ae want steak again.

"Let's ask her where the compound is," Frank says. "She's bound to know." We all nod in agreement.

When Heather returns, she surprises us by bringing three sodas and Frank's beer.

"You just earned your tip." Frank smiles. Heather smiles back. After ordering, Frank asks, "Can we ask you a question?"

Heather sighs, as if she knows what's coming. She bites her lip and nods.

"Can you tell us where—"

She raises her hand to stop him from talking. "Down to the river. Make a left. At the big rock and the trees turn off toward the right. You can't miss it because of the tank. Which just arrived from nowhere. Probably gone next week. But you can't get in there. The whole thing is cordoned off. Really, that's why they call it a compound."

None of us replies.

"We should put up a sign." She sighs. "It'd be easier if we took his ashes and put them in a box by the front door." We all laugh.

The food comes quickly, and Audrey shares her nachos. They're excellent. Frank orders another beer.

"I want to see the tank." Audrey grins.

"Ditto," replies Frank.

"This is stupid," I say.

"Your guy," Frank says back.

"I know. But I don't really want to hang out around here. It's not like there's a grave or anything."

"We have gotten away from our objective, ladies and gentlemen," Frank states in a very deliberate tone. "We have not seen a grave or suicide spot for several days. Let's get back on track."

"Agreed," says Jin-Ae. I grab a nacho and don't say anything.

"Can we go in the morning, at least?" Audrey asks. "I want to walk around and chill out."

"I'm serious, Audrey," Frank says harshly.

"We've been in the car all day. I just want to—"

"What's the point of talking to you? You don't listen to anything."

"Relax. Have—"

"What's the point of anything?" Frank shakes his head. Something about him sounds different.

To my surprise, Audrey doesn't say anything, and we sit in silence for a long minute.

"Fine," Frank finally says, "we're getting a motel."

The words feel like a warm blanket.

Later the sun passes below the tree line, and the temperature drops. I feel like we're really in the wilderness now, far from home. After dinner we drive to the only place that had rooms to rent, the Woody Creek Inn, a big, two-story log cabin with a hot tub in the back overlooking the river. I also feel like we're getting spoiled. Right as we enter the room, Audrey grabs my bag and tosses it, with hers, on one of the beds. Our indoor sleeping arrangements have changed.

I lie down while the others settle in.

May 17

Owen: gay kids kill themselves more than other kids. drink more. use more drugs too

Jin-Ae: nice factoid suicide king. trust me, gay kids just hate themselves more than other kids

Audrey: but we don't hate u. too bad we can't meet somewhere

Owen: maybe its just harder to find lov if u r gay

Jin-Ae: u guys ever come to philly

Frank: no

Audrey: no

I WAKE TO VOICES. THE GIRLS. THE FIRST THING I REALIZE IS that my sneakers are off. One of them did that while I was asleep. My mouth feels dry. Slowly, I roll over.

"What time is it?" I ask, groggy.

"Good morning. Before midnight. Ten, maybe," says Audrey.

"You were tired." Jin-Ae smiles. Turning back to Audrey, she continues whatever they were saying. "I might have thought about—"

Panicked, I bolt up.

"I didn't find it," Audrey interrupts her while staring at me. "What's wrong, Owen?"

"Where's Frank?"

"What?"

"Where's Frank?"

"He went for a walk."

"When?" I shout.

"An hour ago," says Jin-Ae. "I don't know. What's wrong?"

I rub my face. They stare at me.

"Frank brought a gun."

May 21

Frank: do u know why Hemingway shot himself?

Owen: no

Frank: he wanted to be in control. he didn't want to grow old or die from cancer

Frank: and he wanted to go out on HIS terms. not someone else's

Owen: his granddaughter killed herself on the same day

Owen: different year, but same day. she was an actress. margot. margeaux?

Frank: if I was picking one person to meet that would be
*   him. because it's like he took the power. i am always at*
*   someone else's mercy, like my dads*
Owen: he won the nobel prize
Frank: or people saying stuff about me. i hate it. just once
*   I'd like to be in charge. tell other people what to do.*
*   where to go. bang bang*

WE HEAD TOWARD THE CAR FIRST.

"Still here," says Jin-Ae. "That's a good sign."

The door is unlocked. I push the seat forward, reach in from behind, and check under the seat. No gun.

"Why didn't you tell us before?" asks Audrey.

I don't have an answer. I shrug. She punches me on the shoulder.

"You think he's gonna shoot himself?" Jin-Ae asks. "Before . . . before Death Valley?"

"This Hunter guy shot himself," Audrey says. "Maybe he went there, to the compound."

The valley is pitch-dark, except for the lights in the parking lot and the glow down the street from the tavern. No moon out tonight. Together we walk down the dirt road, toward the river. Jin-Ae grabs onto my arm, tightly, scared. I can feel it in the way her fingers don't loosen. Eventually my eyes get used to the dark. The river gurgles steadily. Every once in a while we hear an owl. None of us speaks. I'm too busy listening for a gunshot in the distance. I don't have anything to say, anyway.

Without a lot of towns and streetlights, you can see the stars better than in the city or the suburbs, like in New Jersey. They seem to go on forever. I have never seen that many stars. They calm me down for some reason. I hope Frank is walking around, looking at the constellations and not putting the gun to his head.

We walk and walk. Jin-Ae's grip doesn't loosen. Her fingernails are sharp through my shirt. We find the army tank. Heather, the waitress, wasn't kidding. The tank sits there next to the road, at this turn off, where a big wooden fence blocks another dirt road. The sign says, KEEP THE HELL OUT. THANK YOU.

"Think he found a way inside the compound?" Audrey asks.

Jin-Ae and I both shake our heads. Audrey walks over to the tank. She touches the treads, as though making sure it's real. Then she climbs up onto the front, grabbing the barrel with both hands.

"Somebody should stay here," she says. "In case he's inside or in case he comes back."

I notice the small sign next to the tank that says OWL FARM. Even in the dark I can see the lettering clearly. An animal cries from the woods. We all jump.

"Well, it's not going to be me," says Jin-Ae. "Wilderness is not my thing. That's why I sleep in the car."

"I'll stay," Audrey says. "I want to stay."

"Fine with me, I want to go," replies Jin-Ae.

I want to stay with Audrey. I don't think she should stay out here alone. Neither of them budges in their decisions. Sometimes they can be stubborn. We all can. That's one of the traits of seriously suicidal people I remember hearing about from both Sherri and Mr. Clark. I remember that phrase: "seriously suicidal." I thought that was funny, because that means that there are some people who aren't serious about suicide. I remember Mr. Clark telling me how suicidal people pick killing themselves as an option, and then they won't listen to anything else as a way out, nothing else. It takes drastic measures to change their minds. That was how I ended up in the hospital. I guess the people who aren't serious adjust their thinking better, or quicker. They're the kinds that don't need to be in an institution. Not like us.

AUDREY LIES BACK ON THE TANK, LIKE IT'S A RECLINER.

"Go," she says.

"You should come with us."

"Go."

Jin-Ae squeezes my arm. "Owen, come on." She tugs.

"I'll be fine," says Audrey. "Frank might show."

Jin-Ae and I walk off. I keep turning around to glance at Audrey, who puts her hands behind her head. I imagine that she's looking at the stars and thinking about how small and insignificant we are down here. We're little ants on a pebble, hurtling through space. Jin-Ae walks quickly, almost pulling me along. We don't walk far before the tank and Audrey are too dark to see anymore. Jin-Ae holds my arm the whole way back.

"One of us should wait in the room," Jin-Ae says as we turn a corner and see the lights of the inn. Her grip loosens a little. I don't say anything, but walk her toward our room. "And we should see if he took the car keys."

Jin-Ae isn't like I've seen her before. She's more anxious. I don't know if she's worried about Frank, or bothered by the woods at night, or both. She fumbles with the room key, so much that I take it from her and open the door. She heads straight for the bathroom and turns on the shower.

I look around for the car keys, but don't see them. I bend forward, reach through Frank's things, feeling for the jingle of metal.

"No keys!" I shout to Jin-Ae.

She doesn't answer. I lean in the bathroom doorway, peeking inside. Steam from the shower billows out. "Jin-Ae?"

"Why don't you go find Frank," she mumbles, not looking

at me. She's scrunched up, in a ball, squatting on the closed toilet.

"You okay?"

"Just waiting for the water to boil. Burning shower. One of the only things that helps when I'm totally freaking out."

I'm not sure how to respond. "So," I whisper, "you want anything?"

"Yeah," she replies, sarcastic. "I want to be bulimic, but the vomit grosses me out."

I want to speak but don't.

"Forget it, Owen," she continues, still not looking at me. "Go find Frank, okay?"

"The keys aren't here."

"Check the car. The ashtray or glove compartment. Even under the seat."

"Do you—"

"Go. Please."

I step outside to the parking lot, and feel more alone than I have in months.

May 23

Frank: the kids from columbine are on the suicide website

Jin-Ae: u mean that school

Frank: yes, they shot themselves after they killed
   everyone else

*Owen: i dont think they should count as celebrities
    just b/c they killed other people*
*Audrey: agree. they only became celebrities after they
    were dead*
*Frank: must have wanted attention worse than anyone
    i ever met*

As soon as I open the car door, I spot the gun.

The muzzle sticks out from under the gas pedal. I feel my stomach relax. The gun probably slid out from under the seat while we were driving. Once more, I pick it up, still surprised at the gun's weight. The parking lot is empty. No one watching. Time goes very slow. Something feels familiar, something dark. I notice so many details. I spin the cylinders. The metal clicks in rhythm. I slide into the driver's seat, which is sticky. As I close the door, a huge moth flies toward the lights of the motel.

The metal feels strong, stronger than any metal I've ever felt before. Powerful. People murder other people with guns like this, I think. They rob banks. They shoot squirrels. They kill themselves. I put my finger through the hole and against the trigger. I let my index finger press gently against the sliver of steel that shoots the bullet. I wonder how much pressure it would take to fire the revolver.

I could do it. I could do it now.

In slow motion I lift the gun and press it against my right

temple. The metal feels cold. My hair shifts and makes a soft noise. I wonder where the bullet would exit. Would it go through my head and out the roof or the window? Who would find me? Jin-Ae or Frank?

I pull the gun from my head, slide the barrel into my mouth. The flavor is acidy, metallic. I rub my tongue on the lip of the hole. Audrey pops into my mind. I can taste her.

Why am I doing this?

I don't want to.

I'm crying. My hand shakes. I lower the revolver.

All of a sudden I'm seeing my dad. I want to say something. I am so mad. I can practically hear his voice. I point the gun at the windshield. I squeeze. *Click.* Nothing happens. *Click. Click.*

It doesn't work. Broke. No bullets. I throw it on the seat next to me.

Then I feel the sobs start. I lower my head onto the steering wheel.

Suddenly the horn sounds. I jump, trembling, knowing I have to get out of the car. As I open the door, I spot the car keys at my feet. I scoop them up, then I grab a few napkins. I don't want to touch the gun again, but I have to put it back. With the napkins, I lift, and then slide the gun back under the driver's seat. I slam the door, and run as fast as I can.

I RUN TOWARD AUDREY, HER SMELL, HER SHAVED HEAD, HER everything. Fast, down into the dark, away from the car and the gun. The river sounds closer, louder than before. I listen for owls and anything else, but the river is relentless. So is the noise in my head. I want to hear something, to see something in the shadows, anything to distract me from the gun. The stars seem fewer, darker. I'm not in good shape. My lungs hurt. My legs feel heavy. I keep going, running as hard as I can.

Then my foot catches. Maybe a rock or a hole. The road meets my elbow, knee, chin, and hands. I bang my nose. I see lights. For a moment I'm stunned. My palms sting. Bleeding makes everything else seem less important. I close my eyes and lay on the ground catching my breath, grateful that I've fallen.

I CHANGE MY MIND ABOUT GOING TO AUDREY. I REALIZE THAT I need to locate Frank. I find him in the tavern a few minutes later. He's drunk, again, sitting at the bar, talking to Heather. The two guys next to him look like regular mountain men, with scruffy beards and dirty jeans. I notice that it's past midnight on the plastic, dancing Elvis Presley clock. Seventies music plays. I don't know the song or the band.

"Frank," I say.

He turns to look at me.

"What happened to you?" Heather asks, her hair now hanging down, ponytail gone.

"I broke his nose this week," replies Frank.

I reach up and wipe my chin, wondering if dirt is stuck to my face. The two guys look over as well. Heather shakes her head. "You're a mess," she says.

I notice my body trembling now, in pain, starting to feel the shock of falling.

"You hungry?" asks Frank. "They got wicked good nachos."

I notice the bottle in front of him. He's slouching over, slurring a little. His eyes seem glassy. He lifts his beer and drinks.

"You all right, Frank?"

"Are you?" interrupts Heather. "Have you seen yourself?"

I head to the bathroom. In the mirror, my eyes look purplish. Maybe Frank did break my nose. I touch it gingerly. The sting is greater than I expect. Heather is right: I am a mess. The bruise on my forehead from when I banged my head on the ground is yellowing around the edges. Not that it's big, but it *is* noticeable. I have dirt smears on my face, made worse by the tears; mud, really. Sand and pebbles are stuck in my chin, and a piece of skin is scraped off. I know that will ache later. Of course, I haven't wiped the dust off my clothes. My hands are raw from landing on the road, also rubbed sore and skinned.

For some strange reason, I hear Mr. Clark talking to me. He says, "Drinking water will help you ground yourself, especially if you're in a panic."

I stick my mouth under the faucet and swallow heavily. Then I run my hands under the water. The soap stings, but I like the feeling, anyway. I make the water as hot as it gets. With a paper towel, I wash off my face and the dirt from my head. I bite my arm, hard. Still here.

At the bar, Frank chews nachos. Heather has moved away, talking to other people. A baseball game is on the television, the Dodgers, extra innings. My brother Jimmy hates them. I don't know why. Frank sees me.

"Want some?" he asks, pointing to his food.

I shake my head. "I'll be back." He nods and turns to watch the game.

I run past the car, back to the inn. Inside, Jin-Ae sits on the bed, holding her knees. She looks awful, hair wet, wrapped in a towel. Right away I see the claw marks on her arm, the fresh red scrapes from her fingernails. She covers up with a pillow, neither of us saying anything about the cuts. Everything feels like it's falling apart.

"Well?" she asks. Not a word about my scraped face. I've forgotten that I went to find Frank and the gun.

"Gun's in the car. Frank's at the tavern," I reply.

She closes her eyes, sighs deeply. Out of the blue, I realize what we have to do. "Pack up," I say, "we're leaving."

"You're kidding." Jin-Ae reminds me of a puppy now, sad eyes.

"Pack for everybody. Just throw everything in bags. It doesn't matter. I'll be back."

"Why are—"

"Trust me and do it. Okay?"

She sighs again, and then nods in agreement. I smile, weakly, and head out again. Back in the parking lot, I stare at the car for a second. I pull the keys from my pocket. I inhale deeply and hold my breath for a full moment. It takes me a minute, but I slip into the driver's seat and start the car. I know enough about driving to manage now. With my foot on the brake, I turn on the lights, shift into reverse, and back out of the parking spot. I head down the dirt road toward Audrey.

May 24

Frank: so if we want to meet im the only one who can drive?

Audrey: i drive people crazy according to my mother

Jin-Ae: i have a license, but no car. they only let me drive with them in the car

Owen: i tried to drive a golf cart when i was little but i crashed it

A few miles later I spot the tank. Audrey sleeps, soundly, at the front, below the cannon. She doesn't hear the car pull up, or the door slam.

"Hey," I say, reaching up to touch her leg. "Audrey."

"I'm awake," she replies.

I forgot how still she could be.

"They made this thing to kill people," she says, sitting up. "It's a big giant killing machine. I wish there wasn't any war. And that I wasn't so goddamned pissed off all the time."

I'm surprised at her words.

"I found Frank," I say.

"And the gun?"

"In the car."

"Did he have it?"

"No. It was in the car the whole time."

She stretches and reaches her hand out for me. I step toward her. "I knew he wasn't going to do it."

"What makes you so sure?"

"Hemingway," she says, hopping down. She comes close to me in the dark, touches my arm. I can smell her again, like vanilla or honeysuckle. The scent calms me. "He's all fixated on Hemingway. He won't do anything before we get there."

She's right. I'm amazed at how smart she can be.

"I want to go swimming," she says. "And I'd love to steal this freaking tank. Suicide by tank in Seattle would be an unbelievable end to this club."

"We're not staying here."

"How come?"

I think about that for a second. "Bad karma?"

Audrey laughs. "What the hell. He was your choice, any-way. What did you do about the gun, Owen?"

I pause a long, long moment. "What do you mean?"

"Where is it?"

"Under the seat."

"Let's hide it in the trunk."

I open the back hatch. "Owen," she says, as light falls on me for the first time, "what happened to your face?"

I take out the spare tire. "Fell," I say, showing her my red palms. "Running. In the dark."

Audrey grabs the gun. "Safety's on," she says, "see." She moves a little lever. "On. Off."

Now I know why it didn't work. She puts the gun in the recessed hole. I place the spare tire back on top of it.

"Good," Audrey says. She leans over and kisses me. In the dark she can't see my scrapes. I can barely shut the trunk.

"Let's jump in the river, okay, Owen?"

Audrey takes my hand and leads me to the creek. Aside from leaving our shoes on the bank, we walk in wearing all of our clothes. The water is freezing. I swear I can feel stars swimming in the water with us. I wonder if the dead guy's ashes are in here.

May 25

Jin-Ae: i asked for your picture on myspace. don't think it's
*   a big deal to know what u look like*

Audrey: so?

Jin-Ae: so kurt cobains picture is not you

Audrey: he's like me. he's part of me

Frank: i thought he was part of some river in seattle

Audrey: funny

Jin-Ae: still want to know what u look like

BY THE TIME WE ARRIVE BACK AT THE ROOM, JIN-AE HAS packed all of our bags. We dump everything in the trunk, right on top of the wet clothes. Jin-Ae says, "Don't worry, I'll get Frank to come." I hadn't thought for a minute that he'd make us stay.

Three minutes later Frank climbs into the backseat with Jin-Ae. He nods to me, like me driving his car is a regular occurrence. I guess he's still drunk. I step on the gas and Audrey puts in a CD. "Songs about suicide. I downloaded them."

The roads are empty, and nobody speaks for hours.

Audrey's Top Ten Suicide Songs

10. "Bed of Razors" by Children of Bodom (about two people who kill themselves)

9. "How to Save a Life" by The Fray

8. "A Day Without Me" by U2

7. "Rock 'n' Roll Suicide" by David Bowie (old school)

6. "Jeremy" by Pearl Jam (about a kid who shot himself in front of his English class)

5. "Everybody Hurts" by R.E.M (A don't do it song)

4. "Candle in the Wind" by Elton John (about Marilyn Monroe's suicide—She was naked.)

3. "Suicide Is Painless" by Manic Street Preachers (theme of the TV show *M*A*S*H*. Corny)

2. "Ode to Billy Joe" by Bobbie Gentry (real old country song)

1. "Waltzing Matilda" by The Seekers (weird Australian song about a guy who drowns himself, so he doesn't get arrested for stealing a sheep)

I AM SITTING AGAINST A TREE NEXT TO ERNEST HEMINGWAY'S grave with my feet on his name. I am most definitely still not okay.

We arrived in Idaho one day ahead of schedule. I drove most of the way. I'm surprised that I knew how to drive and that they let me, even though I don't have a license or a permit. I'm not tired either.

Driving helped me feel better too. Very easy to concentrate and drive. I liked that feeling. I drove until nine in the morning. Then Jin-Ae took over for a few hours. Frank slept until noon. I don't mind that we left Woody Creek, which is beautiful, but not for us. It might have been better, though, if we had all taken showers before leaving.

Today, Frank let me take the car by myself. Reconnaissance mission. Find the cemetery. The others stay at the motel.

Hemingway's grave rests on a very small hill with two trees, one on each side. As far as cemeteries go, I can't imagine a nicer one. Sun Valley is beautiful. The mountains go on and on forever. The river we drove across to enter into the valley is full of rapids for rafting. I've seen river after river—Big Wood River, Warm Springs Creek, Cove Creek, Trail Creek.

Ketchum Cemetery. No big gate like the one in Boston, with that giant castle. No mausoleum like Judy Garland's. Just a low fence and a gate that won't close, let alone lock. There *is* a sign that says, NO DOGS PLEASE. I suppose because of the poop.

You can drive almost right up to Hemingway's grave. The road winds around the side of the cemetery, and then cuts across the middle of the graveyard. His grave is almost the center of the whole burial ground. From the pavement, across the lawn, a dirt path leads to his tombstone. The grass is all gone; just dirt from all of the tourists who walk that thirty feet from their cars to his resting place. The tombstone isn't even a tombstone really. I would call it a slab. Nothing sticks up out of the ground, just a piece of gray stone with letters and numbers. "Ernest Miller Hemingway/July 21, 1899–July 2, 1961." Nothing else. Nothing that says anything about his writing, the Pulitzer Prize, or the Nobel Prize. Nothing about his family, even though there are three of them buried in the same cemetery. There aren't even cigars and shot glasses, like I've read about, that people left at his grave. Maybe the caretakers clean up every week.

There's certainly nothing about suicide.

No pinwheels. No pebbles. Only bones rotting away under the ground.

There is nothing to do here, only sit and wait or be dead. I'll tell Frank to bring whiskey and cigars later. When I get back to the motel, I'll also tell them what else I want to do before I die.

May 26

Owen: u wouldn't believe how many famous people
   committed suicide

Audrey: u do your research don't you?

Owen: yes. did u know that nero killed himself?

Audrey: tell us all the ones that you found interesting
   professor suicide

Owen: socrates—philosopher

Owen: hannibal, the general not the killer from the movies

Owen: freddie prinze, an actor

Owen: van gogh, judas, superman

Audrey: superman did not kill himself!

Owen: the old one, george reeves did

Audrey: r you sure it wasn't kryptonite

Owen: that's not funny

Audrey: neither is killing yourself, u suicide obsessed
   maniac

They have food in the room when I arrive. Pizza, fries, and a hamburger for me.

"Find it?" asks Frank.

"Ten minutes, if that," I reply. I spot my bags on the bed farthest from the door.

"Good." He grins, offering me a beer.

I decline.

"You ever gonna have one?"

"Maybe with Hemingway," I reply with a mouth full of food.

He laughs. I swallow, and feel courageous.

"We found the gun, Frank," I blurt. I expect him to look surprised or be angry. He hardly seems to notice what I've said. Frank takes a swig of his beer, reaches for a piece of pizza.

"Did you hear him, Frank?" Audrey asks. "We found the gun."

"So?"

"Were you going to tell us you brought one along?"

"Why?" he asks her, taking another sip of beer.

"It's a gun!"

Frank stays so calm, it's scary. "So?" he says. "I thought we might need it."

None of us says anything. I see the burger in my hand, shaking.

"Christ, this is real, isn't it?" Audrey eventually whispers. "I mean, no messing around."

"We made a deal," Frank says.

Audrey sits down on the floor in the bathroom doorway. She seems paler, except for the scar. "I'm not going to let this happen."

"Let what happen?" says Jin-Ae.

"Group suicide," she replies. "Or murder, maybe."

"I'm not shooting anyone," says Frank, making an outlandish face.

"What a sorry lot we are," Jin-Ae declares, plopping down on the bed next to Frank.

He lifts his beer again, offering one to the others. "Anyone?"

Jin-Ae takes one. Audrey shakes her head no. After a brief pause, I take another bite from my hamburger. My stomach growls, maybe from nerves, maybe hunger. I didn't know that you could be hungry and not hungry at the same time.

"Maybe this is when we decide," says Jin-Ae. "For real."

Audrey stands and then walks across the room.

Jin-Ae continues, "Loyalty to the pact."

"Loyalty to the pack," I say without speaking, a whisper to myself.

Audrey sits herself at the foot of the bed. Jin-Ae tips back her beer. She drinks half of it without taking her lips away from the bottle.

"I'm not," Audrey says. "That's just the way it is. It's stupid." She glances at me.

"You can't speak for everyone," says Jin-Ae. "I'm not much better than when we left. Maybe worse."

"I have to," Frank replies. "Just to . . . just to prove I can do something. Like a man."

Our eyes dart from person to person.

"Owen?" Audrey asks.

My mouth hangs open in midbite. I don't know how to answer.

"Hell!" shouts Audrey, angrier than I've seen. "You ain't doing anything today. Any of you. Got it?" She looks each of us in the face. "And your gun is gone, Frank. No blowing your brains out at Hemingway's grave."

Frank rubs his face, like he's tired. I can tell he's annoyed but not going to do anything about it.

"That wasn't my plan, Audrey," he says casually. "I already told you. Do a few shots. Smoke a cigar. I'd smoke a joint if I had one. We signed a freaking written contract in New Jersey about the end."

I reach out my hand toward Audrey. She pulls away. "Eat your burger!" she exclaims. "What the hell was I thinking when I came on this trip?"

"You wanted to go to Seattle," I reply softly, "and finally finish what you've been trying to do. At least that's what you said."

"What I wanted," she says, "was to get away from my family."

Jin-Ae finishes the rest of her beer in one long gulp. She motions for Frank to hand her another one.

"This is worse that my stepfather's crap," Audrey yells. "We're still going to Seattle. And don't any of you mess that up for me."

Frank and Jin-Ae are in midexchange of beer. They nod, in unison, as though agreeing with her. Very deliberately, Audrey turns to look at me, asking without saying a word. I can't promise, but I want to. I nod.

Suddenly she shouts, "And why are you eating meat if you're my boyfriend for this trip?"

Frank laughs out loud. I put what's left of the burger down and slide on the bed closer to her. She stares at me, brooding. I grab a piece of pizza. I stare back at her and intentionally take a bite. Her face softens. The room is now divided into two beds: the drinkers and the vegetarians.

"I have an announcement to make," I proclaim, surprised at my own voice. I feel stronger than I have in years, maybe ever. "I've come up with something I would like to do before I die."

Jin-Ae leans forward. "No kidding."

I smile and look at her. "No kidding."

Turning, I reach out for Audrey's arm. This time she doesn't pull away. Her eyes make the difference. "I would like," I say, "to visit my brother's grave."

WE END UP, AS A GROUP, WALKING TO THE STORE, SO FRANK can buy more beer. He also purchases a bottle of whiskey and a small box of cigars. Jin-Ae grabs a few bags of snacks: potato chips, pretzels, cheese puffs. She says to Audrey, "I'm going to eat meat." Then she waves a package of Slim Jims in front of Audrey's face. "I'm not your boyfriend."

I've never had a girlfriend before, and it's very interesting to hear someone joking about me in that way.

"Carnivore," Audrey murmurs, knocking the food away from her.

"How the hell can you be a suicidal vegetarian, anyway?" asks Jin-Ae. "That makes no sense whatsoever."

Audrey turns away, raises her middle finger over her head.

"Peace and death," replies Jin-Ae, "whatever."

Audrey insists on renting a movie for the night. None of us is willing to fight over what film to watch, so we let her pick. Audrey chooses *Titanic*, which I saw once when I was little. Most of what I remember is the ship sinking and that the movie is very long. Frank has never seen it. "I know how it ends," he jokes.

We walk back in the dark.

The pizza is cold, but I like it like that, anyway. The fries go untouched. Frank tosses them in the trash.

After I take a shower, they're ready to put on the movie. I forgot how much suicide and death is in that film. First, Rose wants to jump off the back of the ship, but Jack saves her. You can't really change your mind when you jump off of a ship in the North Atlantic, in the dark. Jack talks her out of throwing herself over the railing. Then later one of the passengers decides not to try to get in the life raft. He's this rich man who sits down and drinks a glass of wine while the ship sinks. In one scene, the ship is sinking, and a mother tells her children to go to sleep while she tells them a story. I count that as suicide too, because if you are not fighting to live when you could, then that is like trying to die.

With all the lights off, we're almost having a slumber party. I don't remember having a sleepover with kids since I was in first grade. I did go on that peer-leadership retreat Mr. Clark suggested, but that was a campground with bunk beds and chaperones. Being on your own is different.

Audrey and I lay on our stomachs, next to each other, with our heads where our feet should go. Our faces are much closer to the television that way. I like lying next to her. It's at least the third time I've done that this week. I never thought I would have a girlfriend. I don't think I ever wanted one, but I like how she's a little bossy (like about the vegetarian thing). I like how it feels to be able to touch her arm, and lay next to her, and even more. I never thought I would be with a girl like that, either! I don't know if we will do that again, but I'm glad we did once, at least. Sometimes I'm not watching the movie. I'm looking out of the corner of my eye at Audrey. I don't know any other girls with buzz cuts. Hers looks so good. I close my eyes and imagine her face. I want to burn her image in my head.

After a while the air conditioner chills the room. Audrey pushes next to me. I feel her warmth. Eventually I pull the bedspread up over us both.

Most of the time, Jin-Ae sits on the floor and Frank stays on the other bed. He doesn't drink as much as I expect. The worst scene in the movie is one I don't remember until I see it again. One of the sailors shoots a passenger, then he puts the gun to his head and kills himself. It happens very quickly. I flinch under the covers. Audrey throws her arm over me. I feel like crying.

I don't know why, but I miss my dad, too. I wonder if I will ever cry about him. Suddenly I'm very aware of how much I have cried this week. I don't remember crying at all for years. I cried in the tent with Audrey, and in the car with the gun, and I think another time. I'm not used to all this emotion.

Frank and Jin-Ae, with their clothes on, climb under the covers. By the time the movie ends, I'm exhausted, probably because I haven't been asleep for days. Everyone else, at least, napped in the car. When the lights go out, Audrey rolls up next to me, real close. She whispers, "Shh," in my ear, then she kisses me for a really long time. We don't do anything other than kiss and hold each other, but that's enough for me. I sleep better than I have all week.

Jin-Ae's Top Ten Suicide Legends

10. Hitler offs himself in a bunker
9. Socrates drinks hemlock
8. Japanese guy hari-karis himself on live TV
7. Marilyn Monroe kills herself after the president dumps her
6. Lady jumps off the Hollywood sign in California
5. Judas hangs himself
4. Actress drowns herself in a toilet
3. Buddhist monk sets himself on fire to protest Vietnam War
2. Nine hundred people drink poison Kool-Aid in South America
1. Romeo and Juliet kill themselves because they lack cell-phone technology

May 28

Frank: think we'll ever meet in person?

Audrey: hard for me to drive anywhere since i'm 15

Owen: i found quotes about suicide for our club

Jin-Ae: suicide is a permanent solution to a temporary problem—straight from ms. z's health class

Owen: i looked them up in a quote site, online by someone named camus

Frank: lets plan some way to meet

Jin-Ae: lay it on us

Audrey: who is camus?

Jin-Ae: writer

Owen: "as soon as one does not kill oneself, one must keep silent about life."

Frank: don't like it

Audrey: me either

Jin-Ae: keep looking professor

MORNING. "OWEN," SHE WHISPERS.

I've fallen asleep again.

"Owen?"

I feel myself stir, pull the sheet up.

"Don't look at me, okay? I mean, don't roll over."

My back is to her. I must have turned in my sleep.

"I want to tell you something, but I can't if you look at

me." I can barely hear her. She doesn't want the others to wake.

"All right," I say softly.

She puts her hand on my back.

"I haven't been with anyone in a long time, Owen." I feel myself wanting to turn, to roll over, to kiss her again.

"I haven't been with anyone because—" She pauses.

I imagine she will talk about her stepfather and how hard it was to be molested and have him go to jail. She sighs deeply. Then she curls up behind me, arms over me.

"I had a relationship last year."

I feel her shaking, like a soft cry.

"You're the first person I have been with since then. I didn't want to be with anyone after that."

"Audrey, I—"

"Shh. Don't say anything."

She squeezes me.

"I didn't really jump off the roof, Owen. I made that up because I wanted to do it then. To kill myself." She shivers behind me. "Don't be mad."

"I'm not."

"I just want to be with you now. The way you never kissed anyone before. I want to be with you, because you're so innocent."

Those words seem so strange to hear. I have never

considered myself innocent. I can hardly explain what it means to be wanted.

"My old boyfriend, Ryan, was . . . He left me after he met some girl at a party and forgot about me. I made up a lot of—"

"I won't forget about you," I say, rolling over. Eyes puffy, she looks beautiful and sad.

"You can't say that."

"Yes, I can. I promise."

"People break promises," Audrey says, trying to hold back tears. She moves, and I end up with hands on her shoulders.

"I won't forget about you." I lean my nose into her neck.

"But I—I'm a bad person, Owen. You don't know. I lied about—"

I kiss her. I want her to say more, but I want to kiss her first. To stop her from being sad. Then she doesn't say anything else. So we kiss again, and lay there in each other's arms. I rub her scalp and hair and scar and cheeks until we both fall asleep.

May 30
Audrey: hey all, i'm back
Jin-Ae: where u been
Audrey: hospital
Jin-Ae: wat 4?
Audrey: tried to kill myself again

Jin-Ae: ?

Audrey: but my family doesn't know

Jin-Ae: how does your family not know that u tried to kill
   yourself if u were in the hospital?

Audrey: i'm a good liar

Jin-Ae: how do you lie about that?

Audrey: i made it look like an accident. was in a way

Jin-Ae: nobody tries to kill themselves by accident. u either
   plan to do it or u don't

Audrey: i don't think i was really suicidal. just mad, like at
   myself, self-destructive

Jin-Ae: what happened?

Audrey: i hit myself in the head with a frying pan a few times

Frank: enuf to go to the hospital?

Audrey: yeah, knocked myself out

Jin-Ae: u don't bash yourself into unconsciousness with a
   frying pan ACCIDENTALLY!

Audrey: tru. but even the cops think it was a burglar

Jin-Ae: bull

Audrey: no kidding. they had to cut off all my hair. got a big
   scar too

I WAKE UP ALONE, JUST AFTER NINE O'CLOCK. THEY ARE GONE.
I take another shower and inspect all my bruises. On my face
alone, I have a yellow knot on my forehead, dark purple bruises

on my nose and under my eyes, and pink scrapes on my chin. My hands are cut up.

I eat another piece of pizza, even though it's been sitting out all night. I don't care. I'm hungry. *Titanic* is gone, so I know where they are and, even though a worry passes through my head, I know that they are coming back for me.

I turn on the Sci Fi channel. Old *Twilight Zone* episodes. At least an hour passes before they return. Jin-Ae carries in a six-pack of soda and box of doughnuts. Audrey brings a plastic bag.

"Presents," she says. "For everybody. I brought them from home. We wear them because we're going to Seattle today, eventually."

The drive, straight through, will take at least twelve hours. Audrey opens her bag and pulls out black T-shirts with "Nirvana" written on the front. She's allowed to be creative. Kurt Cobain is her choice, her ritual.

Audrey tosses me a shirt, then says, "Pack up. Picnic breakfast with Mr. Hemingway this morning before we leave."

"Have something planned, Frank?" asks Jin-Ae, bending to pick up her already packed bag. She lifts her Nirvana shirt, holds it up in the air, and rolls her eyes. I realize that she's been wearing long sleeves since we left Colorado. Frank and Audrey might not have seen the marks on her arm. As the counselors at Hastings said about cutters, "The blood and scars are visceral and disturbing." I like those two words. Jin-Ae stuffs the T-shirt in her bag.

"Stogies and Jack." Frank smiles, pointing to the cigars and bottle of whiskey. He and I put on our shirts. Jin-Ae does not.

"Do I get the gun back?" Frank asks.

"Not today," Audrey replies smugly.

"I could go through your stuff to get it," he says. "While you're sleeping. Maybe I already did."

"You didn't," she says. "Or you wouldn't ask for it. Anyway, Owen hid it out at the cemetery yesterday . . ." She looks at me, bringing me into the lie. "So maybe you'll get it when we leave. Or maybe we'll abandon it here. We'll just have to hike ourselves to extinction in Death Valley."

"It's my father's gun," Frank says forcefully. He looks at me, shaking his head angrily.

Audrey raises her voice. "He's not going to want it back after you blow your brains out."

"She's got you wrapped around her finger, Owen."

I don't know what he means.

Loading the trunk, I imagine the revolver under the rug under the spare tire. We cram a few things into the trunk that we won't need today, including our backseat pillows and blankets. I grab licorice and Pop-Tarts wrappers, soda cans, and napkins from the floor, and then dump them in the trash. Hemingway wants us to show up in a clean car.

I point the way for Frank to drive. The graveyard stands empty, not another car around. Cemeteries can be so peaceful. How come the rest of life isn't like that?

Jin-Ae's phone rings right as Frank parks. She grabs the phone from the console, glances at the number, and makes a face. "My mother."

"Don't answer," Audrey says.

Frank opens the door. He looks off at the path and trees. A second ring.

"I have to."

"Why?" Audrey asks. "What's she going to do, come get you?"

Jin-Ae looks at the phone again. Frank leans over, grabs my extended hand, and helps me out.

Third ring. Jin-Ae seems panicked.

"Seriously," Audrey says. "What can she do to you? You're in Idaho for God's sake."

Frank reaches for his box of cigars. "Anyone have matches?"

"I do." The phone rings again. Audrey leans over the front seat and grabs the phone right out of Jin-Ae's hand. "Give me that."

"What—"

"Sorry, wrong number. I'm a lesbian!" Audrey shouts into the phone. She slaps it closed, and then tosses it back into the front seat.

Jin-Ae screams.

"Problem solved." Audrey smiles. "Time for breakfast."

Jin-Ae clenches her hands. Very slowly and softly, she says, "You shouldn't have done that."

"Why? Open the door. Let me out. What's she going to do, yell at your grave? Get over it. Get a life. However many days are left of it."

Jin-Ae doesn't move. Audrey slides across the backseat, climbs out the driver's side door. Jin-Ae picks up the phone, turns it over in her hands.

"Call her back if you're that freaked out," Audrey says, leaning in the window. "Or come have a couple shots with us. Nobody should make you scream like that unless you're having sex."

I have to hold back a laugh.

"Damn, we don't have any shot glasses," says Frank.

"We can make some out of tinfoil," Audrey replies.

"Grab the doughnuts, Owen."

They rummage around in the trunk until they find the foil. Together, we walk off toward the trees and the grave. Audrey holds a blanket and a few other things. Over my shoulder, I spy Jin-Ae sitting in the car. I can't tell if she's on the phone or not.

"C'mon," says Frank.

The car door slams. Jin-Ae follows behind us.

June 1

Frank: what if we each pick someone famous who killed
    themselves and then go visit their graves together?
Audrey: road trip. kurt. seattle. let's go
Jin-Ae: nice idea. too far
Frank: no really. i think i know how to do it
Audrey: how?
Frank: my parents are going to Germany for a month, right
    after school ends, for more like six weeks. i can take the
    car and drive us
Jin-Ae: to seattle?
Audrey: like i said, let's GO
Frank: listen jin-ae, for real. it would take some work, and
    maybe some luck, but we could do it
Audrey: YES! please get me out of this hellhole where i live
Frank: even seattle
Jin-Ae: that's nuts
Frank: IDK. i think we could do it. really. meet in person
Audrey: PLEASE. i'll go. i'll go now

HEMINGWAY'S GRAVE LOOKS THE SAME AS IT DID YESTERDAY.
That's the thing about being dead and buried; nothing changes,
ever.

Audrey spreads out the blanket for a picnic. Just doughnuts and whiskey. Then I see Pop-Tarts, two peaches (I don't

know where she found them), two leftover pieces of cheese pizza, and a Slim Jim for Jin-Ae. She also unpacks a six-pack of beer in bottles.

Frank stands over Hemingway, looking at the letters. He bends down to touch them. Right then I become aware of the date on Hemingway's grave. All this time I have been blocking it out, I guess. July 2. Today. That's one day before Forrest died. July 3. Forrest will be dead for nine years, tomorrow.

I notice a few cigar ends that I hadn't spotted yesterday. They're next to one of the trees. The people who come here, I wonder, do they all want to kill themselves? Why do people visit graves of dead people they don't know? Why are we? I think there's something I want one of the graves to say to me, but I don't know what.

"Well, Frank?" Audrey asks after all of the food and drinks are out.

He turns and nods. "Shot glasses." They mold four out of foil. Then he pours the whiskey.

"Beer chasers," he says, opening a beer and putting it on the grave. "For those of you with poor constitutions."

With a big show of drama, Frank passes out cigars to each of us. Jin-Ae and I both take them but with faces of disgust. Audrey sticks hers in her mouth like a pro. "Tony Soprano." She laughs, chewing on the end.

"Don't inhale," warns Frank. "You'll barf."

"Great," I reply.

It takes a minute, but he lights all of our cigars. They're hard to light.

"Papa Hemingway," Frank begins like the speaker on a stage. "I did think about giving you a twenty-one gun salute—"

Audrey deliberately blows smoke toward him, taunting.

"But my friends stole my gun, and I didn't bring that many bullets anyway."

I drag on my cigar. The smoke tastes gross.

"Ernest—after such an adventurous life, I hope you're happy now," Frank continues. "Live how you want, die how you want."

Frank passes out the whiskey shots. I tell them I'm not going to drink, but Audrey hands me the bottle cap, like it's a minishot glass.

"To Papa Hemingway," Frank says.

Whiskey tastes like fire. Crappy, smelly fire. I don't know how anyone can drink it. Whiskey burns. I gag when I take the capful. I feel it in my nose. They all burst out laughing.

"Here," says Frank, bending, then handing me the beer. "Drink."

The beer is almost as bad. I spit that out.

Audrey and Jin-Ae start laughing so hard that they have to sit down. Frank shakes his head. I toss away my cigar and reach for a doughnut. When Audrey stops laughing, she hands me a soda that I didn't know we had with us.

We all sit down to eat. Frank chugs a beer.

"No drunk driving, Frank." Audrey tosses a piece of Pop-Tart at him that bounces right off the top of his beer bottle.

"No sex, Audrey." He smirks.

She grimaces. I feel myself blush. I pick up a sugared doughnut and turn to look at the mountains. They would be nice peaks to look at forever.

"Where is your brother's grave?" Jin-Ae asks.

"San Francisco," I reply. "We lived there when I was little."

"Isn't that where your dad is now?"

I pause. I don't like to think about him. "He went back there when he left," I say. "I wish I could get him to tell me why he did that."

"Ask him," say Frank and Audrey at the same time. They stop to look at each other, giggling.

"He won't say."

"You asked him?"

"He doesn't answer, ever. Cards. E-mail. I've left him voice messages."

"Jerk," blurts Audrey, who then changes her tone, softer, "if you ask me. Even my dad, in jail, who I never see, sends a Christmas card."

"What was your brother's name?" Jin-Ae asks.

I have a hard time answering. I look toward Audrey. She won't help. I see it in her eyes. She thinks it's good for me to talk about this, to get it out of my system.

"Forrest. He died when I was seven. He was fourteen. Drowned."

Audrey nods, barely noticeable, but I see the kindness in her eyes, which helps a lot.

"That's so sad," says Jin-Ae.

"I was there," I say, surprised that I want to keep talking. "And I couldn't help. I thought it was my fault."

I grab the Jack Daniels bottle and take a mouthful. Again, I gag, this time coughing the whiskey out my nose and across the blanket.

"Whoa, cowboy!" shouts Frank. They all lean back to avoid the spew.

Then Audrey touches my arm, softly. I grab my soda and take a long sip. "I wish I could bring him back," I mumble. "Really."

Frank pats me on the shoulder, like a big brother would do, like a father might do, like a friend. "Want another one, partner?" he asks in a fake Texas drawl.

Even I laugh at that one.

June 2

Frank: i needed someone to talk to once, so i called the
   suicide hotline

Jin-Ae: me too

Frank: i hung up before they answered

Jin-Ae: no way. me too—when they said hello

"Hey," says Jin-Ae, pointing. "Frank has mail."

Sure enough, tacked to the tree is a plain, white envelope with "Frank" written on it. Jin-Ae pulls it down.

"What the hell?" Frank says, looking at the envelope, then at us, then about the cemetery. No one else around.

"Open it," Audrey prods.

Slowly Frank pulls off the end of the envelope. A big cigar and a note. He unfolds the paper, scans it.

"It's a blunt." He laughs. Then he lifts the cigar to his nose, and grins.

"How'd it get here?" Jin-Ae asks.

Frank reads out loud. "'Dear Frank, We found your journal online. Here's hoping you make it on July 2. Have a good day. The Hemingway Society at the University of Idaho.'"

He holds the note out, so we can all see.

"Did you post our route online?" asks Audrey.

Frank shrugs, nods. "Not the end."

"Guess you're a celebrity now, too." Jin-Ae laughs. Audrey reaches into her purse and pulls out her matches. I don't smoke with them, but I do finish one whole beer.

June 2

Frank: isn't there someone's grave you'd like to visit? a suicide. u know, suicide club. that would give us a purpose

Audrey: then we could all off ourselves when we were done. at the same time

Jin-Ae: that's a bit much, audrey

Audrey: in death valley. think of the symbolism jinae. doesnt that appeal to your literary nature.

Jin-Ae: sylvia plath is literary. i would like to see her grave

Frank: we could go there

Jin-Ae: i don't know how i could ever go, not with my parents. they're so strict

Frank: think about it

Jin-Ae: this is crazy, but okay

Frank: im serious. we come up w/ a real plan

Audrey: YES. tell me when. i'll pack 2nite

Frank: owen, u got anyone u want to visit in the cemetery?

Owen: no

Frank: well, go look at that website and pick someone. and u have to figure out where people are buried, and make a map for us too. that's your job

Audrey: here's to a death valley dead end

Owen: i'll never get permission to go. i never ran away before. never even drank

Audrey: we'll help you lie, boyfriend

Frank: just find someone on the list

Jin-Ae: we'll get u drunk later

ANOTHER LONG DAY OF DRIVING AND NIRVANA SONGS. EMPTY country, but at least the scenery is beautiful. Because everyone else drank too much, I'm behind the wheel again for a long time.

Top Ten Worst and Stupidest Ways to Commit Suicide

10. Pretend to have a gun and shoot at police

9. Smother yourself with a dry-cleaning bag (me)

8. Join the army

7. Jump off the roof of a house (Audrey)

6. Lick an electric socket

5. Slit your wrists with a plastic knife

4. Smoke, and wait for cancer

3. Stand on a hill in the rain with metal coat hangers and pray for lightning

2. Overdose on laxatives! (should be #1)

1. Listen to Nirvana in a car until your brain turns into Jell-O

SEATTLE.

True to the rumors, it's raining this morning.

I wonder if it will rain after we die. When you kill yourself, you don't know what happens next, afterward.

None of us talks about what to do tomorrow. I wish I could feel good about going to see Forrest, but I still feel funny. Will we be there tomorrow?

When you kill yourself, you don't have to worry about tomorrow. But when you live, like after you try to kill yourself, that's when you do have to think about tomorrow and the next day. I wish, in a way, I could be alcoholic, like that speaker from AA who came to the peer leadership retreat. "One day at a time," he said. "That's how I make it from one day to the next." I wish I could think like that a little better. Take it easy and not worry about anything except today. He said if you do what you have to do today, all the tomorrows have a way of working things out by themselves.

So today there are certain things I want to do. First of all, I'm going to find flowers for Audrey. I'm sure there are flowers around the whole state of Washington somewhere.

I'm also going to tell her that I'm willing to get a tattoo with her if she wants. I don't have anything in mind. Maybe a wizard; Gandalf. But maybe Audrey wants a snake for me.

I haven't said a lot to her about being my girlfriend or how much I have liked that for the past few days. I'm not sure what to say to her. I don't know how serious she feels about me, or how much is pity, or how much is because we're away from home and getting ready to die. Maybe she just wants a boyfriend, any boyfriend. Truthfully I don't care. Whatever she thinks or feels, I don't have control over. I just like her. I like being with her. I like having a girlfriend even if the reasons aren't good or don't make a lot of sense. And I like sex too. Even one time is enough for me to know why it's so special for people.

I want to call my mother one more time. Last time.

James will look after her. Since my father left, she hasn't been the same. She doesn't work regularly. She doesn't eat well. I know that I cannot help her or fix her, but I can call her. Tell her to stop worrying about me, for good.

Lastly, and I know the most important, is to decide for real and for true, if I'm going to kill myself. This has been going on for so long. I have to decide if I'm going to do it. Or if not, then I need to do something else. Anything else.

Audrey wants to go see Kurt's house. And then she wants to go to the Wishkah River. I bet people go to his house all the time, like a pilgrimage, like when Frank's dad took his family to Graceland. I don't know about the river. Kurt Cobain's ashes were thrown in the river, so where exactly do you visit? Where they were thrown? What about the other ashes, the ones Courtney Love had or lost? How do you visit someone who has no final resting place? Maybe they're as restless as when they were alive.

Maybe I'm so philosophical today because that's what happens to people when they think, and I mean, really think, about the end of their life, their existence. Even if it's almost the last day of my life, I want it to be a good one. I want to live well today.

To start, I would like flowers for Audrey.

June 3

Jin-Ae: sylvia plath is buried in england. that blows the trip don't u think?

Frank: idk

Jin-Ae: can't drive there, can u?

Frank: isn't there someone else?

Audrey: u don't have to go

Jin-Ae: i'd like to go but my family would go crazy and now i don't know what to think

Audrey: owen found someone to visit

Jin-Ae: who

Owen: hunter thompson a writer, in colorado

Audrey: all of u with the writers. do all writers kill themselves?

Jin-Ae: y'd u pick him

Owen: we had a dog named hunter that died when I was real little

Jin-Ae: sorry

Owen: hunter thompson died february 2005. his ashes got shot out of a cannon, like fireworks

Jin-Ae: there's no way i can go

Owen: i figured we could go to that town. his grave is everywhere

Audrey: kurt was creamated. put in a river

Frank: see 3 of us picked people. u gotta come

Jin-Ae: how r u all getting permission?

Audrey: my mother said i could go

Jin-Ae: freaking amazing. frank, u still want to visit hemingway's grave?

Frank: i want to get drunk and smoke a cigar there!

Jin-Ae: i'll do some, but no cigar

Audrey: yes!

Jin-Ae: wats the website so I can look someone up

IN THE CAR, AUDREY POINTS OUT THE SIGN THROUGH THE RAIN. "See. Welcome to Aberdeen," she says. "Come as you are. That's Nirvana."

"Only heard you sing it and play it twenty times this week," quips Jin-Ae.

"Don't you mean twenty times today?" says Frank.

"Oh my God, I can't believe I'm really here!" Audrey shouts. I haven't seen her this restless and excited ever. Not even when she ate that joint in New Jersey.

Aberdeen isn't Seattle. It's south and west, down-river, not the city. Actually, the town looks like any other town—houses, roads, and stores. I think there are more poor people here than in Cherry Hill, which has lots of college people. Most of the houses are smaller than the ones where we live, ranchers and cottages. But it looks, mostly, like any other town to me. Not to Audrey, though. She's perched on her seat, kneeling, head out the window. She's now just a crazy teenage kid, I think. I wish I was like that now too, not suicidal. Only I have something that feels dark inside of me. Ever since Hemingway's grave, it's been back.

"Let's go to the river first," Audrey practically yells. "We can start backward. There first, then where Nirvana played, his school, his house."

"Freaking sightseeing tour," says Frank. "I thought we were visiting graves."

"You went to a stupid football camp and a baseball game. Don't be an ass," Audrey replies.

Frank doesn't say anything, just keeps driving.

June 4

Jin-Ae: if we go, big IF, what do we do

Frank: go visit the graves

Jin-Ae: and what? put flowers on each one?

Owen: its like a quest

Frank: dont muslims all go to mecca once in their life

Jin-Ae: yes. i know what u mean, a sacred pilgimage

Audrey: we go listen to the dead. suicide tour

Jin-Ae: and the finale?

Audrey: u dont really have to ask do u?

THE RIVER DROPS OFF BELOW US, A LONG, SLOW SLOPE OF GRASS, maybe two hundred yards away. At the bottom, I spot sand, not quite a beach, but a place to stand. Maybe that's where they dropped Kurt Cobain's ashes. We're downriver somewhere on the Wishkah, where one-third of Kurt floated away on the current. The car bumps on the mud until we get to a small turnaround where the street, if you can call it that, ends. The wilderness again.

As Frank parks, the rain slows to a drizzle.

"Picnic!" chimes out Audrey.

We know it's useless to say anything about the rain.

Jin-Ae steps out of the car first. She's relented and wears her Nirvana shirt, like all of us. The scratches on her arm seem tiny compared to the other day. Audrey bounds out and runs a few steps toward the river. "Let's go down there," she says.

Frank pops the trunk, so that we can pick out food. Then he and I climb out, slowly. Audrey keeps running toward the water. I grab a bag with warm soda. Jin-Ae starts to gather up one of our blankets from the trunk when the rain bursts, harder again.

"You've got to be kidding." She sighs, looking at the two of us.

I shrug.

Audrey, howling in the rain, runs into the river below us.

"We gotta go," says Frank, surprising me with his willingness. Maybe he thinks he owes Audrey because of the sports things. Jin-Ae rolls her eyes and exhales deeply. I laugh. Frank grabs Jin-Ae's hand and pulls her. They start down the hill, trunk open, leaving the blanket on the ground in the mud. The downpour erupts. I drop the sodas, slam the trunk, and take off after them.

I saw this TV show once on trance dancing, and Audrey looks like the people in that show, spinning, arms out, shouting and moaning. She's missing the long dress and flowing hair, but she's making up for that by splashing the water. The rain helps. She's about knee deep in the river. I start to make out her words. A long, drawn out, "Kuuuuurt."

I sprint downhill trying to beat Frank and Jin-Ae. I am fast and pass them, but I stumble. Fortunately when I fall, I land on the grass. I taste mud. My tumble kicks up pebbles and weeds. I come to a stop in a little ditch. Nothing new hurts this time, thankfully, only the old bruises. Frank howls, laughing. Then, Jin-Ae tumbles, rolling, purposefully I think, past me.

"I meant to do that." I grin at her. Audrey hasn't stopped spinning and shouting in the river. The rain turns relentless, harder than I've ever seen. Frank pulls me up. Jin-Ae steps into the water toward Audrey.

What else is there to say? We walk into the river and start spinning. Audrey's eyes stay closed. Jin-Ae and Frank start to moan "Kuuurt." I like spinning, feeling the rain and the way my body moves slow motion in the water. I shout, more like chant, "Kurt," over and over. Spin. Shout. Chant.

Again, I'm the clumsiest and fall with a big splash. A rocky bottom. This time, however, when Frank reaches out to help me, he also falls. We sit, neck-deep in the water, shouting, "Kuuuuurt." I shiver. My body shrinks.

I think of the Baptists then, who dunk people underwater. I suppose a graveside ritual is as close to church as we are getting on this trip. Audrey helps me up, and then the four of us hold hands in a big circle. The rain pounds so hard and loud, I can hardly hear the others chanting. I can't see well with the water running off of my forehead.

"Can you feel him?" Audrey shouts.

Frank says something I can't make out, just noises. Jin-Ae seems to nod her head. We spin, walk, and jump around in the water holding hands. I feel cold, but not Kurt. I hope Audrey won't be disappointed in me.

DRENCHED, AUDREY'S BLACK T-SHIRT OUTLINES HER WHOLE body. I can't stop looking at her as we climb out of the river. Everything, from shoes to shirts, soaked.

"My wallet!" Frank yells, pulling the soggy holder from his back pocket.

Water squishes in my toes inside my sneakers. Audrey lays down on the edge of the hill where the grass seems less muddy.

She spreads her arms. "This is unbelievable," she says, eyes closed. Then she opens her mouth, catching raindrops.

"We're going to have to dry out somehow," says Frank. "Hope the credit card still works."

Jin-Ae paces. I plop myself near Audrey watching the raindrops bounce off of her face.

"I should've picked someone else," Jin-Ae says.

Frank twirls his wallet. Water flings off.

"Anne Sexton wasn't first or second on my list. And none of you know any of her poetry."

"None of us know any of Sylvia Plath's poetry either," I reply, shivering.

"I'm never going to have the life I want," Jin-Ae sobs over the sound of the rain. I realize she's been crying for a while, but because of the rain, I haven't noticed. I don't know what she means. Why is she crying? Because she is gay? Or because of her family? Or because she wants to visit Sylvia Plath's gravesite? Maybe because we're done.

"I'm not ready for the end of the trip. I can't go home"—she flails her arms around, pointing at the river—"and I don't want to drown myself in this hurricane."

"Me neither," says Audrey.

Finally Jin-Ae sits down. The muddy ground makes a noise, like a fart. Me and Audrey and Frank all burst out laughing.

"Excuse you," Audrey says, sitting up and opening her eyes.

"That's not funny," Jin-Ae growls back.

We laugh again, only this time Jin-Ae's face cracks a half-grin. "Okay," she admits, laughing, "it is."

Audrey grabs a handful of grass. She chucks it at Jin-Ae. I do the same. Unfortunately I also send mud flying. It whacks Jin-Ae in the forehead. I'm about to apologize when a glob of mud hits me full in the face.

"War!" I hear Audrey shout.

All hell breaks loose for a few minutes with mud and grass and rain. I haven't mud wrestled before, and I don't think anyone should miss it. Even when I get dirt in my left eye, I don't care and keep going. We grab one another, and tumble around. Jin-Ae doesn't wrestle, she prefers throwing mud and grass. Frank smashes a clump of mud right on my head.

"Oh no!" I shout. And, right at that minute, sneak attack. Jin-Ae shoves a handful of grass in my mouth. I spit green.

The best part is the end when I grab Audrey around the

waist, and we roll on top of each other, down the hill, like logs. We come to a stop, holding each other. The war is over.

Frank leans down toward me. He holds his eye open. "Do I have something in there?" he asks. I burst out laughing. His whole inner eyelid is caked with mud.

We make our way to the water, to rinse off. Frank splashes water in his eye. I spit grass many times. Audrey, leaning over, dunks her head under. Then she says, "Let's go see that dead porno chick in California. For Jin-Ae."

She looks at Frank. He's still holding his wallet in his hand.

"What the hell," he says. "If the credit card works, I'm in. We already drove this far. Can you find it Owen?"

I shrug and turn to Jin-Ae. I think she's crying, again. Maybe happy. She reaches down into the river and splashes water onto her face.

"Okay," Audrey says. "New plan. Owen's brother Forrest in San Francisco—"

I feel chill, freeze at the sound of his name. I'm not sure—

"—then Hollywood for the X-rated chick. Then Death Valley."

I can't speak. My throat is suddenly closed to everything. The other two just kind of nod.

"Actually," continues Frank, "can we at least find a Laundromat to dry off our clothes first? I'm freezing."

June 7

Audrey: u know we could be in seattle on july 4.

independence day. freedom. we could all do it

together and be free then

Jin-Ae: i don't know if i want to do it with other people

Audrey: u said we were a support group. support means

help. i could help u all do it

Jin-Ae: Oooo boy

Audrey: i knew u werent serious. i only said that to test u

Jin-Ae: y do u do that?! your so annoying!

Audrey: at least i lie better than u

BACK AT THE TOP OF THE HILL, FRANK PULLS A BAG OF HIS DRY clothes from the trunk.

"We should wash all our stuff," says Audrey. "I'm out of clean things."

We end up changing in the car, girls in the backseat. Everyone winds up wearing Frank's clothes since everything else is wet or dirty. Except shoes, of course. I end up with a New York Jets jersey and a big pair of gym shorts. My legs are cold, even with the heat on high. Frank turns on the radio, searching for a sports station. He doesn't find one.

Audrey looks amazing. She's put Frank's Yankees cap over her head. She's also tied Frank's shirt in a knot, so that it's like a halter top, and you can see her belly. Her green dog tags lay across her chest. Frank's pants are gigantic on her, but she's fixed her pink socks through the belt loops so the pants won't fall down. Jin-Ae's pulled on a big, green-and-white Jets sweatshirt, and has the hood up over her head. I think she's wearing Frank's sweatpants. We're all cold.

Frank drives twenty minutes before we find a Laundromat. Fortunately, a couple blocks over from there is a coffee place. We throw our clothes into washing machines, and head for the café. The rain finally stops.

In the coffeeshop, Audrey grabs a table near the window. The river sinks into my bones, as the saying goes. A long time after we're dry, I still feel cold. Frank buys us all drinks: hot chocolate and coffees. The credit card works. I've run out of money, so has Audrey. Jin-Ae has a debit card with something left, but I don't know what. The door slams behind a lady with her kid.

I search for information on Jin-Ae's Savannah, Shannon Wilsey. It is very weird to look her up because there are naked pictures. I feel like a pervert sitting in front of the computer screen with other people around. I try to shrink those pictures as soon as the images show up. I don't think she's that famous. Made a lot of porn movies, but nobody really cares who porn stars are, at least not their faces. Savannah had sex with famous rock stars, which makes you a groupie, not famous. She killed herself in California, but someone else owns the house now. I can't find where she's buried.

A guy has a shrine to her in Nevada. Eleven hours, 663 miles from Seattle to Orvado, Nevada, and the memorial.

"We can be there tomorrow," says Audrey, looking over my shoulder, "if we drive at night, again."

"Maybe we should," agrees Jin-Ae as she pulls the hood of the sweatshirt up over her head again. "I sort of like sleeping in the car with all of you."

I find the miles for San Francisco. Six hours, 43 minutes, 438 miles from Orvado, Nevada, to San Francisco. We actually could visit Forrest if we went there. But I don't think I want to do that anymore. Better to just go straight to Death Valley.

"I should probably call home," says Audrey.

"Me too," says Frank.

Jin-Ae hands Audrey the phone. "Go ahead."

I write a quick e-mail to my mother while Audrey talks. I hear her speak like she's leaving a message, not talking to a real person at the other end.

My e-mail is short. "Mom. I am fine. How are you? We are in Seattle now. I don't know what colleges are here yet. Nothing to worry about. Love, Owen." No lies in that message.

"No answer," Audrey says, handing Frank the phone.

He stands and walks with the phone to the back of the shop.

"Where to next, Audrey?" says Jin-Ae.

"Porn stars."

"No. I mean, here. Kurt's house? School?"

Audrey lifts her hot chocolate, sips. She leans back in her chair. "We're done here."

Jin-Ae raises an eyebrow. Audrey places her cup back on the table. The Yankees cap tilts down over her eyes. "We went to his grave. That's what we said we'd do. I don't think anything could be better than being in that river. It's like becoming part of him."

Jin-Ae nods. "You could drown yourself in there. Keep up your end of the bargain, plus be with Kurt."

"I drank some of that river," Audrey continues. "He was in that river. Now he's in me. I don't need to see his house anymore. Or drown. I'm staying with the pack."

"You're a little bit psycho." Jin-Ae grins.

"You drink any of him, any of the river?"

"Probably," Jin-Ae replies.

"I ate mud," I say. "Does that count?" They both laugh.

Frank comes back, irritated, phone closed in his hand. "I think I'm screwed," he says. He drops heavily into his chair. "My brother told me that my parents want to talk to me, so—"

"Call 'em," interrupts Audrey.

"In Europe? They tried to call home two days ago. He

doesn't know how to stall anymore." None of us speaks for a moment.

"Shit," Frank says, too loudly for other customers to ignore. The woman at the counter with a baby turns her head and glares. Frank doesn't see her.

"What did he say?" asks Jin-Ae.

"I don't know. Not exactly. He said he lied to them, but that's not working anymore. Or he thinks it won't." He lets out a long, slow breath.

Audrey looks unfazed. "So what will they do? Cut off your credit card?" She picks up her drink again.

Jin-Ae asks, "You think he told them where you are?"

"He doesn't know."

We all laugh at that one. Audrey says softly, "Just tell them you went to look at colleges. Or that you ran away to visit dead people."

Frank shakes his head as Jin-Ae rolls her eyes.

"Tell them the truth," Audrey continues, raising her voice. "Heck, e-mail them. Tell them you're okay. That's all most parents want anyway."

Frank raises one finger, pointing. "That's a good idea."

"Yeah." Audrey grins, tipping the Yankees cap back, off of her eyes.

"Wh—"

"No!" Audrey shouts, standing at the same time, so rapidly

that people in the coffee place look at us. "Better yet. Write them a suicide note."

Frank, Jin-Ae, and me just stare at her.

"True or false. Either way, trust me, you won't get any crap about the credit card."

It was such a good day, I don't know why I'm so sad. I want to kill myself again. I don't know why. I feel like it. I know it is stupid. Especially now since I have a girlfriend and everything is so fun, like that mud fight. I know it won't last, is all. And I don't know how to deal with my emotions about that—just when you think you can be happy. Nothing lasts. Not this trip. Not my family. Not my brother.

I have thought about Forrest for hours now. How we used to have fun together, and I would watch him and his friends playing baseball. I liked to hang out in his room, and he would yell at me for messing with his stuff. But he was only kidding. Forrest was so cool.

The worst thing is that now I think about him differently. Like Audrey said, I didn't kill him. He killed himself. Not on purpose. Not suicide. But he killed himself, by accident, by how he jumped into the pool. It's almost like because he killed himself, he should be part of this club and this trip. I don't know if I can go there. It's too private.

We are going to Nevada now. There is not much out here

in western Oregon. Boring roads, dark, and nothing on the radio. Frank is wide-awake because of the coffee, but the girls are asleep. I wish I could sleep. That is what I always hoped killing myself would be like—sleeping. But I don't know about that anymore. Maybe it's not. Maybe it's worse. What if you can hear and see everything and not move. And you see all the people crying. And you can feel the coffin—that I would hate. I wish I could deal with my emotions, because that is all suicidal people need—to be stronger and more flexible and to cope better with their feelings. People live through things worse than me and never try to kill themselves. Maybe I am weak or a chicken.

No, I know why I am sad. Forrest died nine years ago today. And I didn't do anything about it. Not even call my mom.

FRANK LETS ME DRIVE FOR TWO HOURS IN OREGON. NOT because they're drunk, either. He just lets me. One hill goes straight down for sixteen miles. I have never seen anything that long and straight, ever.

June 10

Jin-Ae: i think people are suicidal because they don't have love
Audrey: what about kurt?
Jin-Ae: exactly. love his music. not him
Audrey: so not true. i love him

Jin-Ae: u never met him. he died b4 your mother was born.

   u only love him from what you heard about him

Audrey: i love who he was and what he did

Jin-Ae: respect his music maybe. glorify. love his attitude

Frank: obsess

Audrey: u don't know what u r talking about

Jin-Ae: no. think about it. we all are like that . . . every one

   of us. we think nobody loves us

Audrey: i've been loved before

Frank: my mother loves me. too much

Jin-Ae: well then maybe we don't have love from where we

   want it

Owen: i luv u all

Audrey: that's sweet owen but we're a bunch of computer

   screens

Frank: i'm a real person

Audrey: yeah, but we don't know each other in

   real life

Frank: we will

Owen: i still luv u

Audrey: maybe that's y u are suicidal owen cuz u don't luv

   people in real life

Jin-Ae: that's mean

Audrey: maybe it's true. truth hurts

Jin-Ae: it's still mean

Audrey: the truth isn't mean. it pisses you off cuz it is the truth

Jin-Ae: i luv u owen and i know u in real life

Owen: thank u

Audrey: the truth will set u free but first it will piss u off

Jin-Ae: did your therapist tell u that?

Audrey: no, my lawyer. when i had to be in court about my asshole molester pedophile stepfather

When I wake up, my neck hurts. The others are singing Eminem.

"Hey, sleepy head." Audrey smiles. I'm too tired to answer.

"He's awake?" Frank asks. He turns up the volume. I know the song, not as well as them. They all sing a few lines together. "'Snap back to reality, oh there goes gravity.'"

I yawn and rub my eyes. The diet soda on the floor, already opened, looks appealing. I take a sip. Flat. Outside, mountains and the high desert fill the distance. Far away, I spot two peaks with snow at the top. Not one building in sight, only telephone lines and the road winding down hill.

"We're close, Owen," Jin-Ae tells me.

"How close?"

"Sign said twenty-three miles."

I nod, still shaking cobwebs out of my head. Audrey leans forward, turns down the volume, real low.

"Listen," she says, "the three of us were talking, Owen."

I yawn again. Jin-Ae turns the volume completely off.

"Before the end of our trip, we are definitely going to visit your brother's grave."

I don't know what to say. They won't understand. "I don't think I want to go there anymore."

"We all agreed," Jin-Ae says.

"We know you want to go," chimes in Frank.

I stretch my neck. The cramp pulls. They are waiting for me to speak. I stare at the mountains outside. Jin-Ae taps her nails. It sinks in: I'm going to see Forrest. I miss him so much. And they are my friends. My pack. They will protect me.

Finally I mumble, "Novato."

"What?" Audrey says, shifting the blanket off of me and onto the floor.

"We lived in Novato. North of San Francisco. About an hour."

"Can you find us directions?"

I nod. My yawns don't let up. I stretch. All of a sudden, I feel tears. I can't help it. They just come. I turn to look out the window, to hide my face. Audrey sees me, though, and leans over. Gently, she wraps an arm around me. I don't say anything. Instead a picture comes to me. I remember my mother sobbing, laying in my bed, holding me. She whimpers, "Forrest," over and over. I remember that night, wishing I could have turned myself into my brother, so that she would stop crying. I suppose any seven-year-old would wish for the same thing. I remember how when I breathed in, she held me so tight that some of her hair would pull into my mouth. She smelled sad. She cried until she fell asleep.

As I'm crying, Audrey picks up the red marker. She uncaps it and, without asking, writes on my leg in big letters: "This too shall pass."

My tears don't stop for twenty-three miles.

June 12

Audrey: how come marilyn monroe isn't on our list?

Frank: do u want to visit her grave?

Owen: she's buried in hollywood

Jin-Ae: she's very famous. how did we miss her?

Frank: no one wanted her

Jin-Ae: i just forgot. we all probably did

Frank: no. i mean in real life. she got crazy and then fired from the movies. no one wanted her anymore

Frank: her ex-husband had a rose put at her grave every week for 40 years

Audrey: talk about love

Jin-Ae: insanity is more like it

Frank: grief

Audrey: now that's profound

Owen: hers is the most visited grave in all of hollywood

Audrey: internet fact finder strikes again

Frank: joe dimaggio never got over her

Jin-Ae: i've heard of him before too. suicide?

Frank: lung cancer

Audrey: that's a kind of suicide. real slow

Frank: joe dimaggio. ny yankees. played 13 years, 11 pen-
nants, 10 world series. 3 time mvp

Owen: 56 game hitting streak

Jin-Ae: how do you know that?

Frank: he's my favorite yankee other than derek jeter

Audrey: the boys have something in common. baseball facts

Frank: does anyone want to go see marilyn monroe's grave?

Audrey: no

Frank: anyone?

Frank: ok. so forget her

THE WHOLE TOWN IS NOTHING. LITERALLY, NOTHING. POPULATION of 251, smaller than Woody Creek. As we drive in, I spot only a few houses, trailers, and mobile homes. I wouldn't call this place a town.

The shrine looks weird. It's a shop, bar, and garage all in one. The next building stands a few hundred yards away. The sign says CASINO with a smaller print underneath reading SAVANNAH'S MEMORIAL. Frank is the only one with adult identification, his phony ID. I wonder if that will be a problem for us. I see dozens of beer cans piled on the right of the doorway and bags of trash in the parking lot. Two trucks stand outside the front door. We're early, maybe ten in the morning. I feel my stomach growl.

I think it is really, really weird to visit a porn star memorial. The weirdest thing we have done yet. Creepy. Savannah's dust or worms by now. I understand a grave. But why would this guy have a shrine? That's like marrying the dead. Way too strange, even for me.

While the others clamber out of the car, I stretch, yawn. I find a plum in the front seat. I gobble the whole thing. I must need sugar and water, something, after that crying. Frank waits outside the car for me. Jin-Ae walks toward the building with Audrey.

"Freaky place," he says. "Guess this is what they mean by ghost town."

I feel shaky, kind of unsteady. The girls open the front door and go inside. On the far side is another door, the tavern entrance. I grab a half-full bottle of water and chug. Then, I toss the plum pit. Frank and me head toward the shrine.

Inside, the memorial is surprisingly bright, lots of lights. I spot the girls right away. No one else is visible. The door shuts softly behind me.

"It's a porn shop," says Audrey, with a kind of whisper. She waves her hand, pointing.

She's right. Videos. Lingerie. Leather stuff.

Jin-Ae stands in the far corner, looking at a glass case. I see a strange collection of stuff: a hubcap, big calendar, a coat and hat, a pair of roller skates, a guitar. She raises her hand and touches the glass. I walk to her.

"It's all her stuff," she says.

I notice the big pictures of Savannah, posters, photos. She's blond. The case runs the length of one wall, around a corner. I glance around it and see a motorcycle in the hallway. A Guns 'n' Roses shirt is tacked onto the wall with a little note about her and Slash, the guitar player. Past the motorcycle, I see the bar. A few slot machines blink in the darker part of the building. The memorial is nothing but a few cases of Savannah's things, a motorcycle, some photographs.

I turn and spot Audrey slipping a video under her shirt. I spin my head, looking for the owner. Not here.

Jin-Ae taps her fingers on the small table in front of her. From the bar, a slot machine rings. To the right of the table, Savannah videos fill two shelves. They look faded, old. Videos, not DVDs. I expect Jin-Ae to say something. Instead we just stand there looking at the collection, the memorabilia. Framed on the wall is Savannah's autopsy report. Cause of death: self-inflicted gunshot wound.

Jin-Ae picks up a pen, and I realize that there's a guest book on the table, the kind you find at a wedding or, I suppose, a funeral.

People write their names, where they are from, a few comments. The last entry is dated June 27, the day we were in Pennsylvania. As Jin-Ae writes, I see a picture of Pauly Shore, the actor, and Savannah. The note underneath talks about how much he loved her. I wonder who wrote that note and how they knew.

Frank and Audrey walk over. "Well?" asks Audrey.

Jin-Ae shakes her head.

"I'm gonna get some beer," Frank says, and walks past us toward the bar.

I reach up and touch the framed autopsy report. Weird.

"Hello," I hear Frank call from the other room, shouting for the bartender.

"Let's get out of here," Jin-Ae says. She slams the book shut. Suddenly she looks around. Without a word, she grabs it. Great, I think, another thief. Audrey laughs softly. Jin-Ae hugs the book to her chest. She heads toward the door.

Outside, both girls run to the car. I know they are dumping their prizes inside. Audrey steps back out of the car quickly, putting Frank's Yankees cap back on her head. She lights a cigarette.

"You haven't smoked in days," I say.

"Nerves." She grins, exhaling. "Never stole a porn video before."

Jin-Ae chuckles, then says, "Bathroom." She heads past us toward the bar.

"You wanna go?" I ask Audrey. She shakes her head, takes another drag.

"What if the cops pick you up for shoplifting?" I ask when Jin-Ae is out of earshot. "Aren't you still a runaway?"

Audrey stares at me, quiet for a moment. "What cops?" she finally says. "And what are they going to do? Call my mom? Send me home. She doesn't care." Her voice sounds angry. "Besides we keep making this trip longer anyway."

I find myself backing away from her, just a step.

"Wait," Audrey says. Then she reaches into the car through the back window, fumbles with her bag. I try to see what she's doing, but I can't.

"See this," she finally says. In her hand, she holds a wallet. "Mom, with husband number three," Audrey states, flashing a photograph in front of me. The picture is small, but her mom looks tiny, littler than Audrey. "She works bad hours, like twelve hour shifts, and"—Audrey flips to another picture—"the boys, Aaron and Adam, are both hyperactive seven-year-olds."

Twins. The picture shows them on a playground somewhere. Audrey pauses, takes a drag on her cigarette. "Mostly, it's a zoo there. I bet she's glad I'm gone. If I could live somewhere else, she'd let me. She told me I was a mistake, anyway."

"Audrey," I say softly, "you're not a mistake. I—"

"Don't pity me, Owen," she snaps. "That pisses me off."

In the distance, I spot a truck coming toward us. I don't speak. Audrey drops her photos back into the car.

"I've never tried to kill myself, Owen," she says, looking me in the eye.

I feel my mouth open. No words come out.

June 13

Jin-Ae: my mother will kill me if she finds out about suicide club & this trip

Audrey: kill u? funny. thought that was your job

Jin-Ae: u know what i mean. strict. i have a 10 oclock curfew on the weekend

Audrey: mine wont care if i'm gone. as long as im not a hassle

Frank: i have to be careful too i guess

Jin-Ae: guess?

Frank: i feel like just telling them so they know i run my own life

Audrey: im already on my own. don't have a curfew

Jin-Ae: lucky

Frank: they'll kno when they find my body

Audrey: they just don't care, if u call that lucky

AUDREY STOMPS HARD ON HER CIGARETTE. THEN SHE PLACES her hand on my arm.

"I never jumped off the roof like I said. No broken legs. No wheelchair. Once I started writing those things about it, I . . ." She trails off. I feel my blood race, something is wrong. Terribly wrong.

"I tried to tell you. In the tent. But you were asleep." Again, she grinds the cigarette butt. "And in the motel."

I remember rolling over and how she stopped talking. The truck from down the road finally passes us.

"Owen," she says, "I got hit by a car. That's where my scar's from. Not that frying pan story I made up. My stepfather never even came to the hospital."

I reach for the car, something to steady myself.

"My father's in jail because he didn't pay child support, not because he molested me. I thought if I wasn't suicidal, you all wouldn't like me."

My legs feel weak. "Audrey, why are you—"

I hear a door slam. Frank walks out of the tavern empty-handed. Audrey closes her eyes, exhales. I know she doesn't want to be interrupted now.

"You can tell them," she whispers, opening her eyes. "I don't care. You deserve to know."

"Did you really . . ." I can't finish my question. I don't know what I want to ask.

crash into me ✳ 221

Audrey nods. "The rest is true, about Ryan. Bad, but true. I wanted to die, I felt so bad, but I made the other stuff up."

Frank kicks an empty beer can as he approaches.

"I just needed someone. You guys were so emotional. Like me," she says. "You're like family. Don't hate me."

Her scar looks different now, less frightening. Frank reaches us.

"Told me it was fake ID," he says, interrupting my thoughts before I can figure them out. "Said his brother-in-law is a cop. Christ, gave me a lecture."

Audrey bursts out laughing. She stares at the tavern door, as if she expects the cops to come out after her. Again, Audrey laughs, loud. She looks at me, waiting, expecting me to tell Frank the truth. Then I laugh too. We can't seem to stop. I feel my stomach jiggling and Audrey snorts. That makes us laugh harder.

"Who would figure," Frank continues, ignoring our laughter, "that a guy with a porn shop would give lectures?"

"Can we get out of here?" Audrey finally asks between hard breaths. Frank slaps the car with an open palm in frustration.

"I'll get Jin-Ae," I say.

My legs wobble as I head toward the bathroom. The tavern is darker than the other part of the store, the shrine. A gray-haired man rises from behind the bar, quickly, startling me. He must have been bending down. We make eye contact.

"You're even younger than the last guy," he says. I can tell he means that I can't buy beer.

"Can I use the bathroom?" I say, my voice shaky.

He points by tilting his head.

I wonder what happens if he realizes the guest book is gone before we are out of here. What kind of Nevada police relative shows up? Is this the man who collected all of Savannah's things? For some reason, I think of Savannah's parents, and wonder why they didn't keep her stuff.

The bathroom is in the back, darkest corner of the bar. I walk slowly, afraid I'll trip on something. As I push the men's door with my palm, Jin-Ae walks out of the other bathroom.

"Do you think her parents were upset when she killed herself?" I ask Jin-Ae.

The ladies room door slams. She shrugs. "That's the stupidest question I've ever heard from you, Professor." Then she walks away.

Something about that comment bothers me, and I feel mad. Real mad. I want to punch the wall or, when I look at my face, the mirror. Instead I think of that bartender. I can't remember what he looked like. For that matter, I can't remember what my dad looked like, either.

All that thinking gets me madder. I jam a whole roll of paper into the toilet. Then, I flush, three times in a row. As the bathroom starts to flood, I steal another roll of toilet paper and head toward the car. Now, we're all thieves.

June 14

Jin-Ae: i have more in common wit u all then my family
Frank: we get along better than mine
Audrey: yes!
Jin-Ae: i think my family doesnt really know who i am
Frank: same
Owen: i dont know who i am
Audrey: gee we're going on a family trip

OH MY GOD, THIS WAS THE LONGEST DAY EVER.

First, we hiked for hours. That was my idea, sort of, but not like it turned out. I said that we should walk around and not spend all day in the car. Frank took us to Paradise Valley in Humboldt National Forest, about an hour away from Orvado.

"If you want to walk around, then we should hike up that," Audrey said to me once we parked. She pointed to a big mountain peak. "We do what Owen wants today." Guilt talk. I think she said that because I didn't say anything about her phony suicide attempts or the other lies. Frank agreed about hiking. I don't think Jin-Ae cared. She took her guestbook with her. I think we all didn't realize how long a hike it would be.

The mountains out here are so different than what you see in New Jersey or back east. So much open space, no people. We only saw two other groups—an old couple near the parking lot and a family with three kids that were all running around. I could tell that they didn't go up the mountain, probably only out of the woods to where the big rocks are visible.

The hike was five miles up to the top. We started in some trees. I thought Nevada was all desert, but this part was all green. We walked on a rocky trail next to a rocky creek for a long time. Once, we hiked through the brush to the creek.

"Watch out for poison ivy," Jin-Ae said.

I took her seriously and stayed on the rocks. Frank just laughed. Then we dunked our heads, because it was so hot. That reminded me of jumping in the river in Seattle, only no rain, no Kurt, and not as fun.

"Look!" Audrey yelled, pointing. A bunch of mushrooms, short brown ones with round tops, in a patch of brown leaves. "Fairy ring."

"What?" asked Jin-Ae.

"Circle. See, they grow in a circle. That means you can make a wish."

We all moved around to get a better look.

Frank spoke first. "I wish I wasn't an alcoholic."

"Wish my family was different," Jin-Ae said.

"Works better," Audrey commented, "if you pick something you have control over."

"It's a wish," said Jin-Ae.

Audrey closed her eyes, like she didn't want to tell anyone what she was wishing for. I bent down and touched one of the mushrooms.

I wondered if they were poisonous. And then maybe if we should make tea or stew from them to all kill ourselves, right then, get it over, do something together and end while it was kind of good.

I kept my wish secret: to die happy.

June 14

Jin-Ae: my parents took us on a family camping trip once

Audrey: so?

Jin-Ae: to the pine barrens. 20 minutes from home. 6 days nuthin but family n hiking

Audrey: got it

Jin-Ae: yeah. enuf to make anybody suicidal

THE BAD PART WAS THE GIRLS TALKING, MEAN. THAT WAS WORSE than the hike.

Jin-Ae walked pretty slow, last in line. She often said, "This sucks." She sweated a lot.

Audrey kept saying things like: "Suck it up," "Quit your

whining," "Hurry up," and "Heel, doggie." Frank carried Jin-Ae's little day bag.

Eventually the trees stopped. We saw nothing but mountains and sky. I felt small.

The trail climbed, steady not steep, but always up and the altitude made it hard to walk and breathe. I could feel my fingers getting cold, and once I thought I was going to pass out. My fingernails turned purple. Good for us that Audrey is smart. She brought along a backpack and sodas and the plums. She brought beef jerky and Slim Jims and Pop-Tarts.

Up top, where the mountain flattened out, you could see way off to the parking lot and the houses really far away. On the other side, the mountains look different, more purple. I couldn't see a road or a town anywhere on that side. I felt like I had an insight, like a therapy moment: I thought if you could see things different, like the other side of the mountain, things must be different.

We sat down right in the middle of the path. The summit wasn't much more than a flat spot about the size of a small car. The path kept going, descending on the other side. We were not going that way. I laid my head down and almost fell asleep. Instead Audrey chucked a plum at me, and I ate with my eyes closed. My feet hurt. I drank water, lying down, with my eyes still shut behind my sunglasses.

"Save some for downhill," said Frank.

"I don't think going down is as hard," I replied. I sat up, then threw the plum pit down the hill.

"I think I am happy," Audrey said.

After a second, I knew what she meant, especially for her.

"I mean, I could die up here and be happy. This place is beautiful. If you have to go, it may as well be someplace like this."

For a minute, I thought she was suggesting finding someplace to jump off, like a cliff. But the path wasn't steep, no sharp drop. Then I thought for a minute that maybe she brought Frank's gun with her in that backpack. But I was wrong. She was plain old happy. She sounded like a regular kid, not someone, I don't know—not one of us. Maybe this was her therapy moment, too. Seeing things different.

Frank looked out at the distance. He said, "I could have added hiking up a mountain to my list of things I want to do before I die."

"Glad you're all so happy." Jin-Ae stood up with Savannah's book in her hand.

Audrey leaned forward like she wanted to say something, but didn't.

"This," Jin-Ae said, holding up the book, "is all bull. I decided I hate her. This is crap."

She ripped a page out of the book. I heard Audrey mutter "Uh-oh" under her breath.

Rip. "People saying how nice the shrine is"—another page came out—"and how they miss Savannah."

She started ripping pages out then, not one at a time, but handfuls, throwing them in the air. Yelling. "I hate her. There's nothing good in here. Nothing about being a lesbian. Nothing about being dead."

The pages started to scatter. None of us reacted.

"I hate her!" she yelled. I heard it echoing down the canyon. I wondered if that family with the kids, or the old people, could hear her.

"Hate her." She tore out another page. Crumpled it. Threw it. "Hate it."

Finally she tossed what was left of the book out across the path and down this long hill. I expected the book to roll, but it skidded to a stop. We all stared at the book and no one said anything for a minute.

"Maybe you shouldn't be gay." Frank broke the silence. "Maybe—"

Jin-Ae turned to look at him.

"I'm serious," he said. I started laughing.

"Oh hell," Audrey replied, chuckling.

Jin-Ae grunted.

"Maybe that's why—"

Jin-Ae angrily kicked a rock at him. It missed, but shut him up. I laughed at that, too. Then she said, "Don't mess with me."

"I'm not," Frank said softly, looking right at her.

Jin-Ae turned away. Frank laid back, put his hands behind his head, and stared up at the clouds. Audrey looked at them both, then at me. She shrugged and laid down too, eyes closed. No one spoke for a long time. Jin-Ae kept picking up stones and throwing them down the hill, aiming for the book.

Finally I said, "Let's go to San Francisco."

No one answered. Jin-Ae didn't look at any of us. I watched her move up in size from stones to small boulders, rolling the bigger ones down the hill. An angry act. The last rock carried others with it, nearly making an avalanche.

In that moment, I realized that Jin-Ae hated herself, not Savannah. Jin-Ae was pissed because the porn star wouldn't be able to save her, especially from herself.

June 17

Jin-Ae: suicide also runs in cultures you know

Audrey: ?

Jin-Ae: japan. hari-kari. death before dishonor. or kill yourself if u have dishonored your family

Frank: is that y u want to kill yourself?

Audrey: she's korean

Frank: i know that. i mean because u think u dishonored your family by being gay

Owen: *other cultures do that too. even here they are trying to legalize suicide*

Audrey: *true. doctor kevorgian. heard about him in social studies*

Jin-Ae: *i'm f'ed up that's all. dishonor. gay. whatever. i don't care*

Frank: *i think that's why i did it*

Owen: *kevorkian*

Frank: *because i will never live up to my family. just being alive is dishonor*

Audrey: *sorry—KEVORKIAN*

Owen: *more white people than black try to kill themselves, do kill themselves. more black teenagers are murdered*

Audrey: *king of facts, suicide boy*

Jin-Ae: *i bet asian stats are thru the roof*

THE SUN SANK BEHIND THE MOUNTAINS AS WE WALKED DOWN. The other cars were gone. We decided to camp in the parking lot; car and tent. Frank tore through the car, looking for food. Night came on quick. While Audrey and me set up the tent, Frank turned on the car headlights, so we could see. Jin-Ae didn't talk or help. She read through the San Francisco guide I downloaded on the laptop. For a change, she was the first one to go to sleep.

"GAY DAY!" AUDREY SHOUTS, POKING HER HEAD OUT OF THE tent. We haven't heard Frank and Jin-Ae move from inside the

crash into me * 231

car. The sun is above the mountains. I can tell it's late, that we've overslept, if you can do that on a road trip. At least I didn't have nightmares.

"We'll do all gay things, Jin-Ae." Audrey grins, talking loud as we walk toward them. The car windows are foggy. Inside, Frank lays sprawled across the front seat. His feet seem huge. On the floor, I spot a few beer cans. I didn't know he had any left.

Audrey taps on the passenger window. Neither of them moves. Jin-Ae lays curled on the backseat. They look dead.

"Wake up!" Audrey yells. The veins in her neck show. She bangs on the window, this time with her fist.

"Frank!" I shout, grabbing the door handle. Locked.

Audrey pounds on the window again, louder. "Frank!"

I yank the car handle, harder. The car shakes, but the door doesn't open.

"Jin-Ae!" Audrey screeches. Her voice hurts my ears. I feel my temperature change, like I will vomit. No movement. They are dead. My fingers pull harder than I have ever felt.

"Audrey," I cry.

Frank stirs, rolling. Audrey slaps the car window. I slowly unwrap my fingers.

"Hung over," I say. Once again, Audrey's palm sounds against the glass. Then the computer beeps from the tent, a warning about batteries.

"Go figure out what we're doing today," Audrey says. "I'll deal with this crap."

I laugh, a cackling sigh of relief, and turn to leave. Then I stop. She bangs on the window again.

"Audrey."

She looks at me. I lean over and kiss her on the cheek. She wordlessly turns back to the car.

By the time we pack up everything, it's nearly eleven o'clock. Food is scarce. Only two Pop-Tarts, one plum, licorice, pretzels, two beers. We split up what we have between us, Frank insisting on drinking a beer to get rid of his hangover.

"Drunk-driving rule," Jin-Ae says, watching him tilt the can back.

"One beer," he counters.

"Guess I'm driving."

"One," he pauses for emphasis, "beer."

Jin-Ae concedes and we head toward the coast.

June 18

Jin-Ae: maybe we should have ground rules, like they do in rehab

Audrey: friggin great . . . rehab road trip

Jin-Ae: shut up! u know what i mean

Audrey: NO, i don't. i've never been in rehab

Jin-Ae: officially, i haven't either . . . just a psych hospital

Owen: what kind of rules?

Jin-Ae: like they have in group—you know, no sex between us

Audrey: that should be easy for the group lesbian

Jin-Ae: is that an insult?

Audrey: a statement of truth

Frank: ever hear about getting along?

Audrey: sorry, i'm pissy again i'm probably going to have my
    period when the trip starts

Jin-Ae: thanks for sharing

Audrey: no problem. rule one: no sex

Jin-Ae: great

Owen: how about privacy?

Jin-Ae: like confidentiality?

Audrey: don't we have that already? no one talks about
    suicide club

Frank: yes

Audrey: how about no drunk driving, frank? profile says u drink

Frank: probably a good idea, but i get nights off

Audrey: fine by me

Jin-Ae: agreed if u share

Audrey: no one kills themselves or tries either. until the end

Jin-Ae: ?

Audrey: it would mess up the trip.

Frank: fair enuf

Audrey: none of u off yourselves until at least seattle. don't mess up my trip

Jin-Ae: no sex, no drunk driving, no killing until the end. fine set of rules

Top Ten Best Ways to Kill Yourself

10. Scare yourself to death with horror movies on Halloween

9. Stage a fake guillotine scene in a play, but use a real guillotine

8. Dress like a tree and hang out in lumber country

7. Will yourself to never wake up from a dream

6. Laser disintegration

5. Instantly petrify yourself into stone with magic

4. Purposefully jump in front of a bullet, stopping a presidential assassination

3. Lay down on the ground in a mosh pit

2. Sex yourself to death

1. Overdose on chocolate

WE DRIVE ACROSS THE GOLDEN GATE BRIDGE. "THIS IS THE most popular suicide spot in the world," I say.

Frank glances at me in the mirror. "I'm not stopping, Your Highness."

I nod in agreement.

Not long after, Frank parks in a garage that lets him pay with a credit card.

Gay city.

June 19

Jin-Ae: ok then, suicide dogs it is

Frank: yes much better name than suicide club. Audrey? yur the picky one

Audrey: great but i aint smellin any butts

SAN FRANCISCO IS LIKE ANOTHER PLANET, NOT PART OF THE United States. There are so many everythings—blacks, whites, Hispanics, Asians, gays. I swear, you can hear twenty different languages by walking down the street. I don't know what they all are: Spanish, French, Russian, Italian, Chinese, Japanese. We head uphill, again. I like all the different noises, cars, languages.

Audrey makes us walk to the National AIDS Memorial Grove. "We're going there because it's on the way to church," she says. Church was Jin-Ae's choice. I don't think any of the other of us cares for that idea, but we're going with her anyway. The gay museum she wanted to visit turned out to be cool, so maybe, I don't know, gay church will be interesting, too.

By now it's getting darker with that San Francisco chill. The park is fifteen blocks away, mostly uphill. Frank looks crappy, eyes struggling to stay open. "Maybe you should drink some coffee," I say.

He nods but doesn't say anything.

"Your family know you drink so much?" I ask.

"They don't know anything," he grumbles in response.

"Perfect," Audrey says when we enter the grove, rows of trees, benches, and small lights. "It's like visiting a grave, only better."

"Not suicides," Frank mumbles.

"Makes you think, though," Audrey replies. "I wonder how many of them did kill themselves because they had AIDS."

"Then," Frank says, "this memorial isn't really for them. This is for people who died of AIDS, not killed themselves because of AIDS."

I nod. He sits down while Audrey jumps up on a bench. "Do you think they name trees after the people? Like, plant a tree in their honor?" she asks.

The grove is about an acre, I guess, like a city block. Different trees. Can't see much, only the path lights and the trees closest to the sidewalks. It's not quiet. Traffic rolls by steadily only a few feet away. Audrey jumps off the bench, runs to a nearby tree. "I wish they did," she says.

"I think you're right about the coffee," Frank finally says.

"If you're that desperate, I still have a bottle of unopened champagne from Chicago, and the joint I brought from home," Jin-Ae offers.

"No kidding?"

"Swear." She smiles, raising a hand as if taking an oath. "In the car."

"I wanted to see The Other Mr. Noodle's tree!" Audrey shouts, running to another tree. "But I don't think they mark them."

"Who?" asks Jin-Ae, moving closer to Frank. I wonder if it's safe to be in the park at night.

"The Other Mr. Noodle. The guy from *Sesame Street*. 'Elmo's World.' He died in 2003. They don't know why. He had AIDS."

"Hello," replies Jin-Ae, "AIDS? That's why he died."

"No." Audrey runs past in the other direction. "Mysterious circumstances they said. Maybe he killed himself. I couldn't find out on the computer."

"C'mon, Frank." Jin-Ae moves behind him, rubs his head a little. "Church is on the other side. One block." He stands.

"Damn!" Audrey shouts. "He was my favorite. Next to Elmo. I liked him better than my whole family."

I spy the steeple through the trees. I don't remember the last time I went to church.

June 20

Audrey: what do u think it's like after u die?

Owen: maybe it's nothing

Audrey: i think that sometimes too. i think nothing would be
good, better than this. here it's too hard

Owen: maybe it is happy. heaven is supposed to be like
that

Audrey: IF there is a heaven. IF u go there

Owen: remember that movie, all dogs go to heaven?

Audrey: no. do u really think it's happy there? all the time.
flowers. rainbows.

Owen: idk. what i wonder is y can't it be happy here?

Audrey: good question. do u think it can?

Owen: i think that is y we are a suicide club. b/c none of us
think we can b happy

Audrey: i've been happy before. it's only that bad things
keep happening to mess it up

Owen: i don't think i've ever been happy. maybe as a kid. i
don't think i feel much of anything

Audrey: happy is out there. but u don't have it. that's the
worst. what u don't know u can't miss

Owen: u r pretty smart

Audrey: no. just happy before

THEY GIVE YOU FOOD AT THIS CHURCH, NOT A LITTLE WAFER LIKE
I remember. You get a piece of bread and juice. Almost a meal.
It's livelier than I expected on a Thursday night, maybe three

crash into me * 239

hundred people. The woman minister wears a rainbow robe. I sit next to Frank, near the back.

"Jesus Christ," Frank mumbles, itching his neck. "This is the worst thing that ever freaking happened to me." He's scratching at bug bites, furiously, his hands going rapidly.

Jin-Ae pokes his neck with a pointed nail.

"Ouch!" he squeals.

"Hush," she says. "This is church. There's only like two little bites." She digs in the other nails of her right hand, scratching.

"Why are we here?" asks Audrey. No one answers, but I think that's a good question. Audrey shifts around, restless.

Frank moves his neck. Then he moans peacefully as Jin-Ae hits the right spot. I can feel myself starting to itch too.

"You know," says Frank, "that really is the question of life. Why are we here? If we had a good answer, we probably never even would have met."

"I meant," says Audrey, "why did we come to church today? Not philosophy."

"Sorry," says Jin-Ae. "I never heard of a gay church. Just church that says gay is evil. I had to come." We all nod.

"Wrigley Field," says Frank. "Pilgrimage."

This church is all happy, full of singing. "I could never live like this," Jin-Ae whispers. "That's why I'm gonna—"

"Move here," Audrey cuts in.

"Kill myself." Jin-Ae's voice seems quieter than even a whisper now, like it lacks power. The choir sings "Alleluia," just like I've heard in my own town.

My mother used to have them say a Catholic Mass for Forrest. I don't know why. That never brought him back or did anything to change things. Sitting in church, the thing I keep thinking and wondering, Is Forrest in heaven or is he in hell?

June 21

Audrey: im really happy we're really going

Owen: happy people kill themselves sometimes

Audrey: mr quiet speaks

Audrey: i'm not suicidal today owen. im happy

Owen: the time when most suicidal people kill themselves is when they are happy

Jin-Ae: what are you talking about?

Owen: depressed people don't have the energy to kill themselves. that's what mr clark said

Audrey: ??

Owen: he said it's not when people are depressed that u have to worry about them. it's when someone depressed suddenly has energy. that means they decided to kill themselves. to act

Owen: and that makes them happy

Jin-Ae: hamlet. 2b or not2b

Frank: happy?

Owen: happy because all the bad things they think will be over soon

Jin-Ae: happy about killing themselves soon, not happy about life

Audrey: i'm happy we're going on this trip. no one is always happy about life

Jin-Ae: i'd settle for once in a friggin while

I ASK MY MOTHER HOW TO FIND FORREST'S GRAVE. I CAN HEAR her stop breathing for a second.

"Forrest?" she asks.

I'm standing outside of a gay restaurant called FAG—Fay's American Grill. I see the others inside, ordering at the counter. The light inside makes them seem to glow. Outside, the sky is completely dark. My hand shakes a little, from the chill, holding the phone.

"Yes."

"You're in California, now?"

"Yes."

"Are you sure you want to do that?"

Jin-Ae's phone crackles in my ear. My mother yawns. It's nearly ten o'clock here. I probably woke her up. "I'm a big boy now, Mom," I reply.

"What about your father?"

I let the silence answer her.

My mother is quiet for a moment. I picture her sitting up, putting on the light. Then she says, "Hillside Cemetery, off of Route 101, north. The cemetery looks over the bay, toward the east. His marker is easy to find, on the right, at the pine tree. There's only one pine tree."

"Thanks, Mom," I say calmly, looking at all of them inside, standing next to one another.

"You sound so grown," she replies. "Call me later, after you go." I think she's crying.

When I enter the restaurant, I spy Frank holding a cup of coffee. They have ordered me a cheese hoagie. "For the vegetarian boyfriend." Jin-Ae laughs.

"I thought we should go to a Giants game," says Frank.

Jin-Ae and Audrey both groan. "I thought we should get you a makeover, Frank," says Audrey. Me and Jin-Ae bust out laughing.

"No, seriously. All the gay guys are good-looking," she continues. "Like, refined. You need to clean up a little."

Frank ignores her. "But the Giants are not in town this week, and it's almost ten o'clock."

"I see what you mean," adds Jin-Ae. "Frank needs to get a haircut and go to finishing school."

Again, we all laugh except Frank. "We should take you to

a beauty shop, get you a makeover . . ." Jin-Ae looks at Frank. She tussles his hair. "And teach you to take care of yourself."

"Actually, we should stay in the city," Frank says, pulling away from her. "Drive to Novato in the morning."

I feel my face redden, that quick. Then I try to clear my throat. A little moan comes out.

"Owen?" Audrey says. They all look toward me.

It's almost time to confront my ghosts.

"You've become a bit of a crybaby this trip." Jin-Ae smiles. I grin and feel the tears, anyway.

The waiter arrives with the food. On cue, my stomach growls. The others chuckle. I wipe my face on my sleeve. I eat like it's the Last Supper.

OMG. It's so late. Four a.m. They all smoked pot in the parking lot. I didn't, but they all did. I drank champagne with them, though. Then Jin-Ae and Frank drank so much that we had to take a taxi to a hotel. We went to a club, I don't know where. A lesbian club. Ha. I've never been to a club before. I drank grape soda and gin, or something that tasted good. Sweet. And we danced! All of us. So much. Jin-Ae danced with girls, and we watched until we had to get a taxi and come here to a hotel because none of us could drive. It is so late. I do not think I have ever been drunk before. I must go to sleep now.

MORNING IS VERY ROUGH. NONE OF US WAKES UP FOR A LONG time. The hotel calls our room at noon to ask if we are checking out. My head hurts hearing the phone ring.

Audrey passes out Advil, no more pretending it's her mother's Prozac, but I don't know where she even got it. I don't think I say anything to anybody. I cannot tell if I am sad or sick.

June 23

Audrey: i can't sleep. i can't wait to go. tomorrow's the day

Frank: can't wait to meet u all for real

Jin-Ae: r we really going to do this?

Owen: me too. i think nothing will ever be the same

Audrey: yes. if u are desperate enuf to kill yourself, u should be desperate enuf to go on vacation first

IT FIGURES IT WOULD RAIN ON THE DAY WE DECIDE TO visit Forrest.

I FEEL MY CHEST TIGHTEN. I CAN'T CONTROL IT. THE BRIDGE.

I remember driving across this bridge many years ago. My father's voice, raging. "You should have done something about that yourself, Dolores!" The windows are shut. The sound feels painful. My mother whimpers. His fist pounds on the dashboard. I grab for my brother James's hand. James slaps my knuckles with the baseball cards that he holds.

"I should pull over and throw you off this bridge!" my father yells.

My mother hunches down. I can feel myself shaking, looking outside, at the water, at the boats way below, at the sun reflecting off the bay and the rocks, the islands, wondering how my mother could survive going off of the bridge.

My father's knuckles look white on the wheel. I close my eyes and hope we don't stop. I open my eyes and Frank is driving. My dad is gone. I realize that I have been holding my breath. I wonder if I would survive jumping off the bridge.

June 23

Jin-Ae: so we all agree. we end it in death valley. how will u do it?

Audrey: does it really matter?

Jin-Ae: 2 me

Frank: i could crash car w all of us in it

Audrey: no

Jin-Ae: no. time to b in charge of r own lives

Frank: deaths?

Jin-Ae: yea

Owen: rope, unless something better comes along.

i thought of this b4

Jin-Ae: pills&wrists both

Frank: probably run in traffic if there is any

Jin-Ae: audrey?

Audrey:?

Jin-Ae: well?

Audrey. WTF! Idk. just hold my breath til
*   im dead*

The dog tag tastes like metal.

"Nervous?" Audrey asks.

I hadn't realized that I was biting it.

"You know," she continues, looking not at me but toward the front seat, "they put dog tags in the mouths of dead soldiers."

"Yeah," says Frank.

"Then," Audrey says, pulling the tag out from my teeth, "they kick their jaw shut with the metal sticking out." She slips the metal back inside my shirt.

Frank finishes what she hasn't said, and what I already know. "It's how they identify the bodies."

June 23

Jin-Ae: think vultures will eat our bodies out there

Audrey: does it matter

Jin-Ae: suppose not.

FORREST'S GRAVE IS ONLY ONE UP FROM THE ROAD. WE PARK right next to him.

The rain feels very soft, barely more than mist. I don't care. I can barely breathe. For some reason, I think: Forrest is not a celebrity. Then I realize he is—to me.

"Last stop," Frank says.

I feel my eyes fill. Suddenly I want to kill myself. I want to die. I want to scream.

"Come on," Audrey says, touching me on the arm. "We can have another picnic of death."

"You're crazy," Frank comments, smiling. Audrey nods in agreement.

Frank pops the trunk. Jin-Ae walks to the back of the car, takes out a crushed bag of chips and a blanket. Frank moves away from us, toward the bay, staring out at the water. I close my eyes, inhale deeply.

"I can't go back," Jin-Ae says.

The pine tree is short, like a Christmas tree. I reach out and touch the needles. Wet. I hope Forrest likes it here.

"This it, Owen?" Audrey asks, stepping toward the head-stone, a plain concrete marker with his name.

Behind me, I hear Jin-Ae throwing things out of the trunk. A bottle breaks. Audrey touches my arm, again. I jump.

"Hey," Jin-Ae cries out. "What's this doing here?"

Audrey and I turn to look at her. She holds up the gun. I can't breathe right.

"I thought you got rid of that," Frank says.

Jin-Ae's mouth opens, and then closes as if she wants to speak. She points the gun skyward, over our heads, past the car. Audrey frowns, takes a step toward her, changes her mind. She reaches her hand out. "Give me that thing."

"Is it loaded?" Frank asks me. I shrug.

Jin-Ae keeps holding the gun, with her finger on the trigger. "Maybe I should kill myself instead."

"Shut up," says Audrey.

I gaze down at Forrest's grave, and then I turn to look at Jin-Ae again.

"Seriously," she continues. "How am I supposed to go back home after this trip?"

My hands start to tremble. Jin-Ae shakes her head. Her hands twist rapidly. The gun shakes up and down.

"Look, drama queen," Audrey says, hand still extended. "Do something else. Don't go back. "

I see Jin-Ae's chest heaving. "Last stop," she says.

Audrey keeps talking, louder. "Death Valley, remember?"

"No," Jin-Ae answers, her voice firm. "This is it."

Something inside of me snaps. "Stop it!" I shout. Suddenly Jin-Ae lands on the ground with a thud. The gun is in my hand.

Complete silence for a moment. No one moves. Even the raindrops seem to stop in midair. Then Jin-Ae nods, the corner of her lips turning upward in a repressed smile. She raises herself from the ground where I've knocked her. Frank grins, walks toward us now.

"You were lying about doing it, anyway." Audrey smirks.

Jin-Ae snorts a laugh. "Yeah, Miss Queen of the Truth. Like you really jumped off the roof and—"

"Owen," Frank interrupts, "I thought your brother's name was Forrest. Who's Robert?"

I turn. There's my father's gravestone.

Without warning, I see him. He's lying on the bedroom floor. The gun is next to his right hand. There's blood everywhere. On the curtains and the floor and the bedspread and his shirt. He's there, still, blood oozing on the carpet.

Retching, I lean over and vomit. I stare at his gravestone.

I remember. I am downstairs in the kitchen. I am home early from school, books in front of me on the table. I remember everything. The shot. The thud. Running upstairs.

Jin-Ae and Frank and Audrey are a blur. I can't see them well, not with the tears. They're talking. Their arms wave.

The gun. I remember. The blood. The red.

Now, I feel the gun and what it means. Finally it's in my own hands if I die. I can't breathe. I hear the others yelling.

"I'll show you how to kill yourself!" I shout. "No more pretend. You open your mouth—"

"Owen!" Audrey screams.

She jumps at me. The gun explodes.

I feel the warmth in my head.

June 24

Audrey: do u think dogs can kill themselves

Owen: depends on their pain and their pack

ACCORDING TO THE INTERNET, HEAD WOUNDS BLEED A LOT.

True. More on that later.

I pulled the trigger. The bullet hit me in the skull. At least, that's what I thought. However, Frank told me later that ricochets usually travel off at an angle. More than likely, a piece of the gravestone, a chip of rock, flew off and struck me. I'm lucky the stone only grazed me, if you can call it that. I have a big, long cut across the side of my head, above my right ear.

"WHOA," SAYS JIN-AE, HER HAND ON THE PASSENGER WINDOW, "even the glass is hot."

"One hundred fourteen degrees outside," says Frank.

"It's seven-thirty at night." Jin-Ae moans.

The desert stretches straight and flat for miles in front of us. Ahead, I spot two prairie dogs sitting off the road.

"Pinky wants to know what you're thinking," Audrey says, wiggling her sock puppet against my ear.

"Nothing," I mumble.

The sock bops up and down on her hand. The black eyes Audrey drew on it are uneven. Pinky looks cross-eyed. Audrey puts the puppet against my neck, pretending to kiss me.

"You're a freak show." I laugh.

"You are," she says, pretending that Pinky is talking to me.

"For Christ's sake," Jin-Ae grumbles from the front seat. "You both are. You even look like each other now."

"Get a room," says Frank.

Audrey pretend kisses Jin-Ae with her sock.

"That's disgusting." Jin-Ae shrinks back, against the car door. "You never washed that sock in two weeks."

"Last week." Audrey laughs.

I stare at my girlfriend. Her hair's filling in a little. Slowly I rub my finger against her scalp and scar. My wound runs on the same side of my head. She cut my hair, with scissors, so we could see how bad I was hurt. Maybe Jin-Ae is right. We do look more alike than before, even with all my extra bruises and scrapes.

"Look." Frank points with his right hand. The desert changes color in the twilight. Before us lie miles of white, the salt flats, long and endless. The shadows turn the desert floor into a blend of colors. The road shimmers from the heat.

"That's why it's called Death Valley," says Frank.

"Bad water," I correct him. "Lowest elevation below sea level in the United States. Total saltwater."

"Know it all," Pinky the sock puppet mumbles in my ear.

"How long to Vegas?" asks Jin-Ae.

HERE'S WHAT HAPPENED. I POINTED THE REVOLVER AT MY father's headstone, and then pulled the trigger. Immediately I knew I was hit. I fell straight to the ground as the gun went off. The bullet or rock splinter smashed into the side of my head. I felt like someone lit my scalp on fire. I reached up and grabbed my head. The blood spurted through my fingers.

"Owen," Audrey cried. She threw herself on me. Frank and Jin-Ae raced over too.

"Pressure!" Frank yelled. "Don't let the wound bleed. Is he—Owen, are you . . . ?"

"Okay," I said, on my knees.

Audrey lifted her shirt over her head. She held it against my scalp.

"Are you sure? Owen?"

Jin-Ae wrapped herself around me then, both arms, pinning my arms in a funny position while I held my head.

"Owen, you can't—," she cried, sobbing. Her mouth leaned against my ear, whimpering.

"Don't you die on us!" Frank yelled. I never heard him so forceful.

Suddenly I grasped what was happening—they were all trying to save me.

I never thought I was worth saving.

AFTER JIN-AE STOPPED SHRIEKING, SHE TOLD ME TO LIE DOWN. Frank said, "That'll make him bleed worse."

They sat me upright. My shirt felt wet.

"Get some stuff," Frank told Jin-Ae, pointing to the car. "Clean up stuff. Band-Aids, blanket." He stared at my eyes, trying to see if I was all right. She let go of me and rushed toward the car.

Audrey yelled at me, at all of us. "No more killing ourselves." Just like that, we made a new pact.

"Didn't mean to," I said, as she pulled her shirt off my head. The bleeding seemed slower. "That was a mistake."

She pressed the shirt back against the wound, harder than she needed to do. "Mistake?" she said gruffly.

"Accident."

Jin-Ae brought over a shirt for Audrey, water, a pile of napkins. My head hardly hurt, but the blood looked awful.

"I'm getting rid of this thing," Frank announced. He

picked the gun up off of the grass where I'd dropped it. We watched in silence as he walked toward the bay. At the edge of the cemetery stands a big boulder, with a drop-off below to the water. Frank climbed up. Then he leaned back and hurled the pistol with an arc, far out into the bay. His form reminded me of all the athletes he never thought he could be.

I wondered what he'd say to his dad about the gun. And what would happen later, when all those credit card bills came. But we never talked about it. I didn't want to wreck the picture in my mind of him standing up there, so graceful, on that rock.

Maybe I'm different now.

I found out another secret, but not about me.

Audrey told me that Frank and Jin-Ae had sex the night we watched *Titanic*. I was fast asleep. Audrey, however, heard them, even though they tried to be quiet. I don't think they are in love. Perhaps they both wanted to try it at least once. I suppose it doesn't matter what form love takes; maybe we just need to take it when it comes.

I called my mother yesterday, too. The conversation didn't last long.

"Hi, Mom."

"Owen." Her voice sang, happy.

"I wanted to tell you I was all right," I said. I didn't tell her about the gun.

"Where are you?" she asked.

By then we were headed toward Death Valley, somewhere on the outskirts of the Mojave Desert, at another gas station pit stop. "On the way back," I answered. "But it'll be a while."

"Good," she said. "I've missed you."

A pause. My turn to speak. "I went to the cemetery, Mom." She waited for me to keep talking. "I saw them both."

Suddenly I felt the tears. I think she heard me catch my breath. Then the conversation turned in slow motion.

"I haven't been there," she whispered, "in a long time."

I mumbled something neither of us could understand.

"Owen," she said, "are you okay?"

I swallowed, pretty hard. "Not really," I replied, looking at Frank waving to me. Time to go. "But I'm better."

So now I want to live.

I know I want to live, because there are things I want now. Suddenly I have many reasons. I want to visit Forrest's and my dad's graves with my mother, and maybe even my brother James. I hope I can say good-bye and move on with my life. This is stupid, but I want to see the girls give Frank a makeover. Also, I want to raft in a river, but not the one near Woody Creek. I want my friends to live, Jin-Ae and Frank and Audrey.

My Top Ten Reasons to Live

   10. Stars in a really dark sky

    9. Driving across the country

    8. Nirvana

    7. My mom

    6. Our dog pack

    5. Gay Bingo

    4. Mud fights

    3. Kissing

    2. Magic Marker tattoos

    1. Pink socks

And I want to see Audrey naked, if she will let me, with the lights on. Not just in a dark tent. With Audrey, I want—

No, wait. Some things should be secret.

Gratitudes

Pals:

Cindy Kelly, Sherri Reissman, Maureen Higgins, Mallory Richter—my first fan club;
and the many family and friends who shared a kind word along the way, especially
Catherine Driscoll and her Jacksonville prayer group.

Mentors and Helpers:

Ellen Hopkins, gracious and talented author who gave more than she'll ever know;
Neal Shusterman, a writer who acted like I was good more than once;
Bonnie Hearn-Hill, who was right when she said the story could live in a single sentence.

Pros and Kindred Souls:

Anica Rissi, my editor, whose belief and begging changed everything;
Andrea Brown, superagent and Vortex of Light who remembered a Red Sox jersey;
Michelle Andelman, critic and angel.

Voices:

Sara Osendowski, who mattered and whose life pointed me toward a road trip;
Brie Pierce, my favorite poet and a muse of sorts;
the young people and their families who have told me part of their stories, including,
but not limited to: Sean, Katie, Liz, Kate, Dana, Dan, CS, Michael, Sarah, Ashley,
Jim, Rob, Justin, Jess, Lauren, Emily, Daniella, Stosh, Chris, Addie Lee, Ian, Kevin,
Nicole, VM, John, Neil, George, Dillon, Justin, Steve, and the hundreds of others.

My Clan:

Loving wife and partner, Elizabeth, without whom I couldn't do it;
one-of-a-kind daughter, Alexandra, who puts up with me with a smile;
exciting and exhausting sons, Samuel and Jonah;
proud mother, Eleanor; and
my not-quite-stepdaughter, Amelia, because love doesn't care about form.

My Source:

God, who, mercifully, blessed me with a second chance many times
and let Owen speak to me.

Albert Borris has tracked snow leopards in the Himalayas, backpacked through Iceland, and skated ultramarathons in Georgia, but his favorite daily adventure is working with teens. Albert is a national award-winning student assistance counselor. In spite of the bad jokes, he chooses to live in New Jersey. Find out more about Albert's writing, his latest adventures, and his top ten most embarrassing moments at AlbertBorris.com.

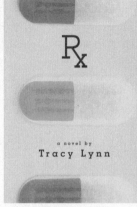

LIVE ON THE EDGE

a novel by Jason Myers

exit here.

JASON MYERS

JASON MYERS

THE MISSION

a novel by the author of EXIT HERE

FROM SIMON PULSE
PUBLISHED BY SIMON & SCHUSTER

SIMONTEEN

Simon & Schuster's **Simon Teen**
e-newsletter delivers current updates on
the hottest titles, exciting sweepstakes, and
exclusive content from your favorite authors.

Visit **TEEN.SimonandSchuster.com** to
sign up, post your thoughts, and find out what
every avid reader is talking about!